THE FAITHFUL ONE

A BILLIONAIRE BRIDE PACT ROMANCE

CAMI CHECKETTS

BIRCH RIVER PUBLISHING

COPYRIGHT

DEDICATION

To all my friends. Thank you for being there through the laughter and the tears.

INTRODUCTION BY LUCY MCCONNELL

I've heard it said that some people come into your life and quickly leave—others leave footprints on your heart. Jeanette and Cami are two wonderful authors and women who have left their mark on my heart. Their overwhelming support, knowledge, and general goodness have pushed me forward as a writer and nurtured me as a friend. That's why I'm pleased to introduce you to their new and innovative series: The Billionaire Bride Pact Romances.

In each story, you'll find romance and character growth. I almost wrote personal growth—forgetting these are works of fiction—because the books we read become a part of us, their words stamped into our souls. As with any good book, I disappeared into the pages for a while and was able to walk sandy beaches, visit a glass blowing shop, and spend time with a group of women who had made a pact—a pact that influenced their lives, their loves, and their dreams.

I encourage you to put your feet up, grab a cup of something wonderful, and fall in love with a billionaire today.

Wishing you all the best,
    Lucy McConnell

AUTHOR'S NOTE

Writing the billionaire bride pact series with my friend, Jeanette Lewis, has been delightful. The original premise and darling cover ideas were all her ideas. When I heard about it, I had already written The Resilient One, minus the bride pact, and I begged her to let me in. Originally, she asked me to write four of the eight brides, but then a couple months ago she asked me to write two more—Trin and Summer.

Trin was originally called The Lost One because she lost touch with everyone. I wasn't as excited to write her story because of that. I love all the connections to the other girl's camp friends, but once I started this story I just fell in love with Trin and Zander. Zander's story made me cry several times and Trin's friend, Moriah, made me laugh out loud.

I hope you enjoy the story of The Lost One who became The Faithful One.

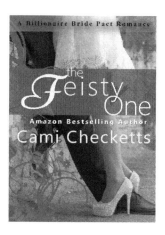

Get your FREE book, *The Feisty One*, from the bestselling Billionaire Bride Pact series, by signing up to be part of my VIP club HERE!

THE BILLIONAIRE BRIDE PACT

I, Trin Dean, do solemnly swear that I will marry a billionaire and live happily ever after. If I fail to meet my pledge, I will stand up at my wedding reception and sing the Camp Wallakee theme song.

CHAPTER 1

The nonstop ringing of his cell phone pulled Zander from his sleep-induced coma. He pushed his hand through the sheets until his fingers connected with metal. "Lo?" he muttered.

"Zander. How are you, son?"

"I feel like somebody smacked me in the head with a baseball bat. You?" He sat up in bed, trying to clear his head. Pulling his phone away to check the time, he sighed. It was four a.m. His dad, an early riser and confirmed workaholic, never seemed to take into consideration the time change from Kauai to the East Coast.

His dad chuckled. "Probably because you work so hard. Everything's okay?"

His dad knew he wasn't accomplishing much of anything but traveling and training to compete in Ironman races. Yet his dad acted like he was proud of him and always treated him like he was fragile. Zander would be annoyed, if he didn't understand.

"Hanging in there." They rarely scratched beneath the surface, both afraid of the emotions that might arise. "How about you?"

"Good, good. Hey, I need you to do me a favor."

"Sure." His dad had given him a huge inheritance and annual annuities that made it pretty fruitless to waste time holding down a regular job. Zander owned a couple of successful businesses that sold everything from training gear to nutritional supplements in the Ironman and triathlon circuits, but he had great people in place to run them and he mostly just traveled, trained, and competed. After he sobered up a couple of years ago his dad had gifted him a six-point-five-million dollar condo in Midtown. That was home when he went home. He hadn't been back to his parent's mansion in Vermont since his mom was murdered ten years ago. No intention of ever returning. He endured enough pain during an Ironman race, no need to set himself up for the emotional version of torture as well.

His dad asked for favors so rarely, Zander always said yes when he could make it work with his training schedule. "What's up?" His head still felt groggy. He regularly woke at six a.m. to train and sometimes five in areas where the heat came early in the day, but four was stretching it a bit. He tried to focus on his father's words.

"Have you ever seen that show Undercover Boss?"

"Yeah." Oh, no. Television shows and him didn't mix. *The Bachelor* had been a huge mistake. Every woman trying to connect with him on any level they could, whether it was throwing their clothes off or trying to psychoanalyze why he hadn't formed lasting relationships since his mother's death. He wasn't sure which of his dad's lamebrain marketers had come up with the idea of putting him on the show in the first place, but then it might've been his dad hoping he'd find a wife and live happily ever after. Must be a curse of parenthood, wanting your children to be happy.

He and his dad had a rare fight after that nightmare wrapped up and aired. They both came to the conclusion there would be no more television fiascos. It hadn't helped that Zander had been plastered most of the show and put off a horrible persona for his dad's brand. His dad owned everything from grocery stores to hotels to toy stores. It was important to him to give a good impression. Huge fail on Zander's part, but of course his dad didn't blame him. He never would.

"Don't worry. I'm not putting you on it." His dad laughed uneasily. "Though I'm sure you'd do great representing us now."

"Thanks," Zander muttered, but he wasn't so sure. Tranquility Woods in Maryland was one of the most luxurious and effective addiction centers in the nation. Zander had come out truly a better person with a faith in the good Lord that had been missing before, but he hesitated to say he was a changed man. He was sober and he was doing semi-productive things, but he still didn't feel like the kind of man he wanted to be, like his dad.

"I want to do something similar on our own," his dad continued. "Nobody but you and I will know about it. It'll basically be a vacation."

He paused and the silence was heavy. Zander's entire life was a vacation and he knew it bothered his dad. His dad worked from five a.m. until eleven p.m. then dropped into bed and started all over again in the morning. The words vacation and relaxation were almost curse words to him. He never said anything about Zander's lifestyle, well, maybe he complained to their longtime cook and friend, Hannah, but he was always kind and patient with Zander. Probably worried he would relapse into alcoholism or worse, move onto hard drugs, if he said boo to him. No, that wasn't fair. His dad genuinely loved him.

His dad cleared his throat. "I think there are some triathlons going on in the area over the next month that you could compete in and it'd be a great place to train."

"Okay. The half Ironman in Kauai is tomorrow then I can fly out. My next full Ironman is the first weekend in December in Australia so I'd have a few weeks at your resort." That didn't sound too bad. He'd go stay in one of his dad's luxury hotels, get to know the staff, and report in.

"Great. I'll email you the info. It's one of my smaller places, a bed and breakfast in Montgomery."

Had he heard his dad correct? He wouldn't really send him back to that area. Auburn was about an hour from Montgomery and he and his mom had flown into Montgomery that fateful trip.

"Montgomery?" he pushed out.

"I know it's tough, son, but you need to face it at some point."

Okay, scratch all the thoughts about his dad being patient. How could he send him back there? The memories whooshed in without invitation and Zander blinked quickly, jumped to his feet and went out on the master suite's deck. The rental house overlooked Secret Beach on Kauapea Road. The sound of the waves usually relaxed him, but nothing could relax him as he tried hard to not think about his mom.

The one thing he did know about his dad—when he had an idea he didn't back down. Maybe that was why he was a billionaire. Zander used to share that quality with his dad. It was the reason he'd excelled at football and been recruited by some of the top D1 schools in the nation during his senior year of high school. He'd quit football after his mom's death, barely scraping out a bachelor's degree as he drank every night to try to dull the pain.

"Anyone in particular I should watch?" He'd do this for his dad and then he'd be done. He'd avoid the demons waiting for him in the nearby town of Auburn and then he'd never, ever return.

"I don't want to tip you off. Just befriend everyone. You're great at that. Like your mom."

A hard knot squeezed in his chest. He couldn't think about her. Not now.

"She'd be proud of you."

"Please don't, Dad." His mom always thought he could do no wrong, but he couldn't remember her without thinking of that night.

"Make her proud. Will you, son?"

Zander wanted to say yes. With everything in him, he wanted to, but he couldn't lie to the only person on the planet who truly cared about him. "I'll try," he squeaked out.

It was lame, but his dad let him get away with it. He'd let him get away with everything short of murder since Zander had found his mom dead and blamed himself.

CHAPTER 2

Trin hurried into the entryway of the Cloverdale bed and breakfast. She felt like she was in *Gone with the Wind* every day in the exquisite southern style mansion. She'd worked hard to make sure that the twelve guest suites were immaculate and always rented. At five hundred to a thousand dollars a night she knew the bed and breakfast was profitable for Mr. Keller, but the billionaire probably didn't care with all the luxury hotel chains he owned and who knew what other businesses and investments. Yet he'd always treated her and the Cloverdale as if they were something special. She hated to think of him as a surrogate father because that was just cheesy, but he was a really cool guy.

He'd personally called and told her about the important guest they had coming to stay. A young man who was going to stay for a few weeks and participate in triathlons in the area while he trained for an Ironman. Trin prayed it wasn't Mr. Keller's son, Zander. She'd watched *The Bachelor*, along with every other besotted woman in the nation. Zander was too handsome for his own good and though he had an understated wit and she'd been impressed with the considerate way he treated all the candidates, it was obvious he was free-loading off his dad and she had a hard time respecting someone like that.

"I finished polishin' the big ole Sunny Suite, those stompin' grounds are cle-ean, not a tassel out of place," Moriah's petite yet shapely form swept down the grand staircase. "It's fit for the queen of Bathsheba."

"I think we need it fit for the king."

"That too. Yes, ma'am."

Trin swatted at her. Children, teenagers, and young adults in the south seemed to have it drilled into them from birth to yes, sir, and yes, ma'am, any adult, even if the person they were addressing was barely an adult. Moriah did it to tease Trin more than anything, but Trin did love the manners the children here displayed.

"Don't you yes ma'am me or I'll dock your pay."

Moriah giggled. "You know I'm the best housekeeper and cook in any county in the state so I don't think you'd better be fixin' to mess with my pay." Moriah laid the accent and sass on thick.

"You watch the attitude, friend."

"I'm a Southern girl. Attitude is what draws the men in." Moriah snapped her fingers.

"I wish I had a little of that sass."

"Naw. You're beautiful just the way you are."

"Thanks." Trin clapped her hands together. "Okay. I think we're all ready. Mr. Keller said this man is a very special guest of his so I don't want to mess anything up."

"Mr. Keller thinks you bathe in wine, bless his heart. His special guest better be on *their* best behavior." She placed a hand on her hip and tossed her black cornrows.

Trin laughed. "Is bathing in wine a good thing?"

"It means you are tasty and intoxicating. Yeah, girl." Moriah threw a hip out and her hands up. A dance move ensued that Trin couldn't accomplish if someone pushed her rear in the right directions.

"Oh, my, goodness." Trin shook her head and hurried behind the large check-in desk. Her open office was directly behind the desk. Her employees teased her about Mr. Keller having a crush on her and it just weirded her out. He was older than her stepdad and was truly like a favorite uncle or father figure.

She tapped on the keyboard to bring up the reservations for the week. The house was full. They had another couple coming in tonight, but everyone who was staying here added to the charm of the place, in Trin's opinion. She hoped their special guest agreed, a Mr. Jason Hunley. Nice name.

The door sprung open and Marcus tugged one bag behind him, shouldering a garment style bag. Marcus winked at her and Trin chose to ignore it. He was a great employee. She'd found him on the Riverwalk downtown. He'd asked her to spare some change. She'd given him five bucks and told him if he could clean up, she'd give him a job at the Cloverdale Mansion. It had been the bravest thing she'd done in a long time, opening her home to someone who may or may not respect it.

He'd shown up a couple hours later. Somehow he'd taken a shower and put on clean clothes. He now shared the refurbished slave quarters at the back of the property with her. They each had their own apartment and she made sure to lock hers every night.

Marcus was a good guy who'd just gotten down on his luck. Trin knew exactly how that felt. If she worried that he also seemed to have a propensity for alcohol and weed, she kept it to herself. He'd only missed work a few days and that was all right. She and Moriah could keep everything going without him. It was just really nice to have him help with yard work and being a bell hop, plus he could fix anything. He'd saved Mr. Keller all kinds of money tinkering with things. She knew above all else the billionaire cared about things being in the black so she made sure to keep it that way.

Walking behind Marcus with an athletic style bag slung over his shoulder was none other than Zander Keller. The air seemed to suck out of the two-story foyer as he focused in on Trin and those smoky blue eyes penetrated to her very soul. His perfectly-sculpted lips turned up in a smile that just radiated appeal. It was like those lips were sucking her in and saying, *You'd give anything to kiss me.* She gave herself a shake. No need to react like a drama queen just because a fine man walked through their door.

Trin broke from his gaze and glanced over at Moriah. Her mouth was honestly hanging open. Trin tried to get her attention, but it didn't work. Yes, Zander was one of the best-looking men on the planet, but they had to be professionals.

Zander walked forward and extended his hand. "Miss Dean? I'm Jason Hunley."

Trin placed her hand in his and plastered on her professional face. Huh? She wanted to spit out something like, *Come again?* Why were Mr. Keller and Zander lying about who he was? His normally dark hair was highlighted and longer than usual and he had a few day's growth, probably attempting to cover that handsome face, but none of it really worked as a disguise. Either he thought she lived under a rock or he didn't really care if she recognized him.

"We're thrilled to have you here, Mr. Hunley." She gestured to Marcus and Moriah. "If there is anything any of us can do to make your stay more comfortable, please let us know."

"Thank you." He released her hand, those blue eyes regarding her solemnly.

"Marcus. Will you please take Mr. Hunley's bags up to his room?"

"Yes, ma'am."

Trin didn't scold him, though she wanted to. Marcus had picked up on the ma'am thing and was rolling with it nicely, though he was from upstate New York.

"Would you like a glass of lemonade?" Trin asked Zander.

"Sounds great."

She walked with him to the north side of the house where a long, spacious gathering room took up the front part of the house with an archway into the large dining room. The kitchen was at the rear of the north wing. That was Moriah's haven.

"Moriah?" Trin nodded to her friend. "Would you please bring some refreshments for Mr. Hunley?"

"Of course. I'm on it, ma'am." Moriah rushed through the gathering area, the dining room, and into the swinging door of the kitchen.

Trin didn't let herself look at him as they walked into the living room and each chose a plush straight back chair to sit in. What was he doing here? Was Mr. Keller checking up on them? Why? He had hotels all over the nation, no probably all over the world. She'd always wondered why he'd taken an interest in Trin's home, bought it from her mom after her grandparents' deaths, promoted Trin to manager, and then sunk exorbitant amounts of money into it. Now she had no clue why he would waste his time sending his son undercover to monitor them. Their reviews were fabulous on Trip Advisor and Yelp and honestly they were too small of apples to even be in the barrel of Mr. Keller's responsibility list.

Her eyes raised to meet Zander's again. His eyes were impossibly blue. Women had described them like the ocean or the sky, but Trin thought they looked like the gorgeous blue butterflies that she used to chase at home in Wisconsin. Smoky blue in the middle and almost gold on the edges.

His face had been sculpted into irresistible manly lines and currently was covered with dark stubble. The recent pictures she'd seen of him were clean shaven, but he'd always had that sexy Hollywood-style stubble when he did *The Bachelor*. Trin couldn't say which she preferred. Both, please. He had a really nice build, but he looked like he'd filled out a little bit since *The Bachelor* as well. She'd heard he had gone through a high dollar rehab not too long ago and it was obvious he was in peak physical condition.

She couldn't imagine how hard it would be to overcome an addiction as strong as alcohol or drugs. Moriah always teased her because Trin couldn't walk away from a plate of cookies and she was pretty sure there were no addictive chemicals in them, but maybe Moriah had a secret ingredient she wasn't sharing.

He smiled at her as she studied him and the room's temperature spiked. My, oh, my. "So, Mr. *Hunley*." Did he think they lived under a turtle's shell? She knew exactly who he was. She wondered if Marcus and Moriah had already figured it out too. "Are you here for business or pleasure?"

"More of an escape." He smiled that devastating smile again and it was all Trin could do to not sigh dreamily. "I'm doing some triathlons in the area and training for the Ironman in Australia the first week in December. My training takes up most of my time."

Trin's eyes widened. A full grown man who spent most of his time training for a race? As she worked most days from sunup until she dropped into bed, that bugged her a little bit. She didn't need a training plan to stay in shape. She could put him to work on the grounds and he'd have all the exercise he needed.

Maybe she should just make him a sign that read, *Non-Contributing Member of Society*, and hang it on his forehead. Okay, that was mean and judgmental. He seemed nice, she'd had that impression when he did *The Bachelor* and tried to let the girls down easily. She remembered the relief, like a boulder being taken off her shoulders when he had chosen a finalist but then later came out and explained that they were not a couple. Which was silly because she didn't know him. She knew and loved his dad, but she'd never met Zander before today.

Moriah brought a tray of lemonade and her Snickerdoodles. Darn her. Trin could never eat only one.

Zander took a cookie and a glass of lemonade, thanking Moriah and giving her that trademark smile. Moriah's dark eyes lit up and she ducked her head in a completely uncharacteristic Moriah move. Normally, she'd be batting her long eyelashes and swiveling her hips. "My pleasure, sir. I hope they tantalize your tasting buds."

Trin rolled her eyes at Moriah's blatant flirtations. She broke a piece of a cookie and placed it on her tongue, savoring the spicy cinnamon, rich butter, and sugar. Yum. "They're fabulous as always, Moriah."

"Thank ya kindly, ma'am."

Trin shot her a warning look. Moriah's throaty laughter rang through the room. Trin swatted at her behind as she walked away.

"You seem to have a good relationship with your employees," Zander said.

Trin raised an eyebrow. "They're my friends."

Zander took a long swallow of his lemonade. "Then you're even luckier."

Trin wondered at the longing note in his voice. The famous

Zander Keller probably had women vying for his attention every second of the day. Surely, he didn't need friends. No, everybody needed friends. Maybe he wanted a real friend, not just someone who wanted his body. But who wouldn't want his body? Darn, she needed to think professional thoughts and stop checking out the striations in his arms.

"What do you do for work, Mr. Hunley?" There she went again, being judgmental and trying to box him into a corner.

"Please, call me Jason."

She pursed her lips. "All right."

He stood and walked around the room, checking out the white mantle above the fireplace framed with bookshelves and then looking through the French doors out at the wrap-around porch and sweeping lawn. Trin loved all the windows in the house, even though they were drafty when the temperature dropped, but for the most part they had great weather so the windows just embraced the sunlight and made her happy.

"I feel like I've stepped back into the 19th century. I love how you preserved the authentic feel of that era yet everything is fresh and clean-looking."

"Why do you assume I did it?"

He shrugged. "It just feels like … this is your house."

She glanced away from him. "It was my grandparent's home. My mother inherited it, but sold it to the current owner, Mr. Keller, after they died. I was already basically managing the house and Mr. Keller," *Your dad*, she wanted to say, "was generous enough to keep me on staff. Helping me finish my degree and allowing me to continue to manage the house that has been in my family for generations." Talk about an info dump. Why did she need to tell him all of that?

He looked sharply at her. "I don't know that it's generosity when you're obviously doing a great job of taking care of the place and keeping it rented. The reviews I read were all glowing."

"Thank you. Mr. Keller has been a blessing for me. He spared no expense refurbishing the home and grounds." She'd been able to be part of the details and it made her so happy—from refurbishing the wood floors to painting the white trim—her house was perfect.

"How long has the home been in your family?"

She didn't remind him that it wasn't in her family anymore, it was in his. She rarely remembered that fact herself. "It was built in 1860 by my great-great-great ..." She half-laughed. "I can never remember how many greats."

"So right before the war?"

"Yes, sir."

"Spoken like a true southern child." He smirked. "So you grew up here?"

"No, sir." She smiled, liking teasing with him, but then her smile slipped quickly as she thought of her childhood. "We lived here until I was five then my daddy died, my mom remarried, and we moved to my stepdad's home in Wisconsin."

"When did you end up back here?"

"I graduated from high school and immediately came back here to be with my nana and papa." No need to tell him her stepdad had given her enough money for a bus ticket and told her good luck being an adult. "Went to Huntingdon College just down the street and helped take care of the house. But Nana had a stroke and passed away my senior year and Papa died a few weeks later." She smiled wistfully. "He couldn't live without her."

She glanced up at Zander. His face had tightened and his blue eyes were cool.

She cleared her throat, guess he didn't want the romance story. "My mom didn't want to deal with running the bed and breakfast, even though I promised her I could do it. My stepdad just wanted the money, so they sold it." Again on the telling him too much and he was lying to her about who he was. A sickening thought washed over her —Mr. Keller didn't trust her and had sent his son in to check on her. Then a worse thought came—Mr. Keller was going to sell the house and had sent his son in to figure out if it would be profitable. She wanted to call Zander out right here and now, but would that force his hand?

"I'm sorry to hear that." Zander's gaze wandered out the windows to the expansive yard and oak trees shading everything. She had one spot at the back of the property for her garden, but everything else was nice and tree-covered.

"It's a beautiful place."

"Thank you. I'm grateful to be here. Don't know what I'd do without it." Now, that was a fabulous idea. Lay on the guilt. They couldn't sell her home. Maybe she'd still have a job if they did, but there were no guarantees, and nobody would be as good of a boss as Mr. Keller. He gave her the freedom to run her house the way she liked and she almost felt it was still hers, as if her grandma would walk out of the kitchen any moment or her grandpa would poke his head in the front door and have Trin snitch him a cookie.

Mr. Keller had sunk a ton of money into the place with renovations, but she knew they were in the black now. Was it making enough money for him to justify those renovations or was he just wanting to sell and be done with such a small property?

She forced herself to smile at Zander. No reason to make him suspicious. "We should get you checked into your room."

Zander stood, taking the hint, holding aloft half of his cookie. "I only took one because I know about southern hospitality and didn't want to offend anybody, but you were right, these are fabulous."

"I always get after her when she bakes those."

"I try not to eat sugar, but there must be exceptions."

Trin eyed him warily. "I don't trust anyone who doesn't eat sugar."

Zander chuckled. The warmth and depth of it washed over Trin. She had to resist fanning her face. Darn southern heat, right? It wasn't him that was heating her up. But it was November and the high today was only seventy. She couldn't really blame the environment for the flush to her skin.

"I'm eating it right now." He took another bite of the cookie and a crumble of cinnamon sugar clung to the side of his lip. "Does that mean you can trust me?"

"You're wearing it right now." Trin reached up and brushed the crumble from his lip. Her fingers seemed to linger of their own accord. His lips and beard were much softer than they looked.

His eyes flashed up to meet hers. She swallowed hard and dropped her hand.

"Thank you," he murmured.

Trin nodded and spun on her heel. Her heels clicked merrily on the tile floor. He followed her to the grand staircase and they walked side by side up it. He ran his hand along the oak banister. "Wow. I just keep feeling like I'm stuck in *Gone with the Wind*."

"You say that like it's a bad thing."

"That show terrified me. I'm waiting for Scarlett to sweep down the stairs and tell me off."

Trin laughed. "I'm scared of spiders," she commiserated.

"And you live in the south?"

"I know, dumb, right?"

"I'll kill all your spiders if you keep Scarlett away from me."

They reached the landing and Zander extended his hand. Trin shook his hand, loving the feel of his strong fingers surrounding hers. "Deal." She pulled her hand back, lest she forget she had a lot of reasons to be wary of this good-looking, lying man. "Women scare you?"

"No, just harpies."

Trin had a flashback to him being on *The Bachelor*. He had gotten rid of any snarky or demanding women as quickly as possible. He'd ended up with some real sweethearts, but they still hadn't made the cut. She would love to ask him about it sometime. If he ever owned up to who he was.

"I'll keep the harpies away." She smiled at him and pointed to her right. "Just down this hall, sir."

"Oh, no, not you too. Everybody in the south calls me, sir, and I have to look around for my dad."

Trin understood thinking only older people should be called sir and ma'am, but she saw an opportunity and pounced. What if she was one of the harpies she'd just promised to keep him away from? She thought how to phrase the question, but settled for, "Are you close to your dad?"

He nodded quickly. "He's good to me."

They reached the Sunny Suite.

"So, this is me?" Zander asked. He leaned against the door and Trin was reminded all over again why women thought he was such a heart-throb. The casual elegance. The perfectly sculpted facial features. The nicely-formed muscles that were large enough to be noticeable, but not bulky. He was obviously quite the athlete. She sighed and then caught herself.

"Yep." Producing the key, she turned it in the lock, swung the door open, and handed him the key.

His fingers clasped around hers with the key between them. "No key cards at the Cloverdale Mansion?"

"No, sir." Her house was old school and she liked it.

He smiled and released her hand. Trin took in a quick breath, reeling from his touch and the look in his eyes. He still hadn't turned from staring at her to look into the room. It was one of her favorites—spacious and sunlit. He should probably check it out and stop checking out *her*.

"Are you pleased with your accommodations, sir?"

Zander cast a quick glance around the huge suite with large windows overlooking the rear lawn and gardens, a sitting area, huge bathroom with the original claw-foot tub and a brand new glass-enclosed shower, the four-poster bed that wasn't original, but was period specific. He refocused quickly on Trin's face. "It's exquisitely beautiful."

She blushed and cursed whatever ancestor had made it so she didn't have beautiful dark skin like Moriah. "Thank you," she muttered. "Please let any of us know if you need anything. There are refreshments available in the dining room at all times. Breakfast is from seven to ten a.m."

She turned quickly and started back down the hall.

Movement behind her made her turn. Zander was leaning against the doorframe again, simply watching her go. She tripped on the rug, but quickly righted herself.

"Are you all right?" Zander's footsteps catching up to her made her increase her pace.

"Fine." She held up a hand and almost ran to the stairs. She needed to get away from his penetrating stares and casually leaning body, and figure out how she was going to save her home.

CHAPTER 3

Zander sprawled out on the bed. It was comfy. He was impressed that he'd made it off the airplane in Montgomery and all the way here, with memories shadowing every step, and he was only slightly itching to open the small fridge in his suite and see if it was stocked with alcohol. Standing, he hurried to the fridge before reason could stop him. He wouldn't drink any of the alcohol, he just needed to know what he was up against. Popping the door open, he sagged with relief. Bottles of water, fruit juice, and lemonade. Had his dad requested those refreshments in his fridge or was it standard to not stock alcohol at the Cloverdale?

He lay back down on the bed and checked his phone for swimming pools in the area. He should have been thinking about training schedules for the next week and how he was going to get the sugar from that delicious cookie out of his system. Always a sucker for peer pressure, he didn't know how to turn those ladies down when they offered the cookie. He was feeling a little sick, but his thoughts were full of the beautiful manager of this little bed and breakfast. She was tall and lean, but not like the working out at the gym kind of lean. She was the lifting, working, and cleaning kind of lean. He loved her hair, a red so dark it was like the rich, cherry wood of the cabinets in his

Midtown condo. She had a straight nose, full lips, kind of a Julia Roberts' look, and eyes that were a deep brown you could get lost in.

He stood and chastised himself. He was here to monitor this bed and breakfast, but he had no clue why. Was his father wanting to sell it? Zander had only been here an hour, but he liked the feel of the place, the employees he'd met, and the spaces he'd seen were obviously well-cared for. He thought about Trin and how her mom had sold this place out of her family. It made him hurt for her. She seemed to think of the house as almost a relative and it was probably her link to the grandparents she'd loved.

He'd never met someone so bonded to their home. Most of his associations were with athletes who traveled similar circuits and they were all focused on training for the next race. Trin was focused on caring for this place and her two employees. Admirable.

Zander had no connection to a place like that, not anymore. He was glad his dad had hired Trin to run this home that meant so much to her. If his dad was wanting to sell he'd have to insist they put in a clause that the manager stayed on staff. But what if those people decided to sell?

He shook his head. He was getting way ahead of himself. There was no telling if his dad wanted to sell or why he'd sent Zander here. He loved his dad, but the man enjoyed giving his son puzzles and letting him solve them. There would be no information coming if he tried to press his dad. He would have to play this out.

One other thing was bugging him. There'd been something in Trin's eyes. An indication that she knew exactly who he was. He glanced in the mirror. The longer, highlighted hair and beard must not be working. Then he remembered. He'd had similar length facial hair on *The Bachelor*. Had she watched that horrid show? If she knew who he was, why didn't she say anything?

He pulled out his razor kit and decided to change his look. He smiled to himself. It might be a little late. He was halfway through shaving when he realized, he hadn't smiled this much in a long, long time.

❄

ZANDER FINISHED SHAVING and thought he'd go find Trin. He was supposed to be shadowing her, right? Well, his dad hadn't exactly said shadow, but something like that. He hoped this version of *Undercover Boss* had cool rewards for the employees at the end like the real show, because right now he'd probably gift Trin the house her ancestors built. He wondered if his dad would approve. Not if he was planning to put it on the market.

He quietly made his way through the house, almost tiptoeing down the stairs. He shouldn't sneak up on Trin, but it would be fun if he could hear what she was thinking.

Making his way through the large living area and then the stately dining room with a table that would seat twenty, he heard voices in the kitchen. Perfect.

He moved as quietly as he could to the door and stood, almost holding his breath. He realized he was smiling, again. What was it about this house, this woman, that made him smile? Not that he was miserable in general, but having seared his pleasure centers for so long with alcohol and marijuana, life seemed pretty dull. Sobriety was not really exciting.

He did enjoy training, competing, interacting with fellow athletes and his employees, and helping his dad when he asked, but he didn't have a lot of reasons to just … smile.

He pressed his ear a little closer and could hear Trin and the other employee, was it Mary? No, it was something more exotic. Moriah. That was it. The dark-skinned girl was a beauty, but she looked about eighteen. Trin was the one that appealed to Zander. He hadn't cared much about women, or really anything, for quite a while. *The Bachelor* had left a bad taste in his mouth. Why any woman would want to chase after an alcoholic just because he was rich was beyond him. It was kind of nice that Trin didn't know who he was. Well, maybe she didn't.

"He's a handsome devil, that's for sure," Moriah said.

"Can't argue that," Trin responded.

Zander grinned again.

"But why is he lying to us?"

Zander about fell over. How did she know he was lying to her? Had she guessed who he was? He leaned closer to the door. It swung inward and he sprawled into the kitchen. Jumping to his feet, he was sure his face was beet red. The two women had flour-covered hands, aprons on, and eyes wide with surprise.

Moriah held a lump of dough in her hand. She waved it at him. "Mr ... Hunley. Are you all right?"

"Yes, thank you." The excuse that he didn't know it was a swinging door would just make him look stupid. They'd know he'd been leaning against the door to try to eavesdrop.

Trin's eyes twinkled with humor as she studied him. "Decided to shave, Za—Jason?"

She knew. Why didn't she confront him? He was going to play along and make her be the one to say something. "Yeah," was the intelligent response he came up with.

"It looks very nice." Trin pressed the dough to the floured counter and rolled it out with a wood rolling pin.

"Nice?" Moriah muttered. "The man is smoking hot."

Zander was sure he was blushing again. He didn't know what to do now. Should he make some kind of exit or could he find an excuse to hang out with the two of them? Today was a rest day and though he usually lifted weights on rest days, he hadn't found a gym yet. He didn't need to do any official training until tomorrow. He could go explore Montgomery, but that wasn't much fun by himself. He was still struggling a little bit with being back in the area where his mom was killed. He'd avoided most of the southern states, particularly Alabama for the past ten years because of the memories. The last thing he needed was a relapse into alcoholism. His dad had been so patient with him. Zander knew soon he'd need to step up and start learning how to oversee his father's businesses, but for now he appreciated that he could focus on his training and the escape that was for him from the bitter memories of losing his mom and being responsible for her death. One day at a time. Getting ahead of himself or trying to do more than he should always made him thirsty for something he shouldn't have.

"Moriah," Trin chastised out of the side of her mouth. "Can we help you with something, sir?" she directed toward Zander.

"I, um." How could he tell her he wanted to be near her, and not just because his dad had asked him to do the *Undercover Boss* imitation. "Can I help *you?*"

Both women's heads flew up from focusing on their bread dough. Moriah particularly was eyeing him like he was a few marbles short. Trin looked to be fighting a smile.

"You're a guest," Trin said. "We don't ask our guests to help us work."

"But I've always wanted to learn how to make … whatever you're making." Smooth Zander, real smooth.

Trin laughed at him. She actually laughed at him. It started as a low chuckle then rumbled up into a full-blown laugh. Moriah stared at Trin for half a second then she started to giggle too. Zander tried to hold it in, but their laughter was infectious. One second he was embarrassed because he'd asked to help and they were making fun of him, the next he was full-on laughing with them.

"Sorry," Trin finally managed to say, "it just struck me as funny that you want to learn, even though you have no clue what we're making."

"It was my lame way of asking if I can hang out with you," Zander admitted.

"Yeah?" Trin cocked her head to the side and gave him the cutest smile. It completely lit up her face. Man, she was a beauty.

"Yeah."

"I think he meant me," Moriah inserted, winking brazenly at him, then starting to chuckle again.

"Um, yeah, both of you." Zander was fumbling for words in a way he never had before. He'd been trained well throughout his life how to react professionally and in a manner befitting his station. His mom and dad had loved him unconditionally, but they'd also prepared him for his place in life.

"Don't lie to the momma," Moriah said and Trin started laughing again.

"You're a mother?" She looked much too young to be a mom. Her dark hair was in long cornrows down her back and her skin was smooth with almost rounded cheeks like a young girl.

"That's right. Got me the cutest little boy on the planet. He stays with my momma while I work."

"Congrats. How old is he?"

"Two. Chubby cheeks like you wouldn't believe." Moriah grinned proudly. "Ooh, just to squish him makes my day."

Zander nodded, not sure what the proper response to the momma should be. He wondered what had happened to the boy's father, but it wasn't his place to ask.

Trin threw him a lump of dough. He caught it on instinct. "Come over here and I'll teach you how to roll them out." She glanced askew at him. "We're making cinnamon rolls for breakfast."

"Shouldn't I wash my hands or something?" he asked.

"Aren't your hands clean?"

"Well, yes, I washed them recently, but I was thinking like food handler's permits and stuff like that."

"We won't be using your dough for the guests. We'll let you eat your own creation."

"Oh, gotcha." Zander had never been such a mess around a woman. She was teasing him and having a great time at it and he was playing right into her hands.

Trin cleared him a spot on the floured surface and handed him a rolling pin. "Roll it nice and smooth."

Zander tried to obey but the dough put up a fight. "Do you usually make your breads the day before?"

"Depends on how ambitious we are. Something like cinnamon rolls takes a while so we don't really want to wake up at three a.m."

"Makes sense. So, what's the hardest thing about running a bed and breakfast?"

Trin gave him that appraising look again. She definitely knew who he was. Dangit. He'd been hoping to stay incognito for a little while longer.

"You a reporter?" Moriah asked.

Trin chuckled and Zander couldn't help but laugh too. "No. I just, um, like to learn about the places I'm staying." Yes, complete fail.

"Gotcha. The hardest thing?" Moriah pursed her lips. "I'd say dealing with customers who don't think nothin' is good enough," Moriah answered for the two of them. Her dough was smooth, and she was spreading what looked like melted butter over it. "I mean, look at how gorgeous this place is and how blessed we all are to be here. It riles me when they complain."

"Do you have that happen often?" Moriah seemed to have a positive attitude even when complaining.

"No," Trin said quickly. "For the most part people are enchanted with the house, and nobody can resist Moriah's cooking."

"That's right, sista. Especially my biscuits and *gravy*." Moriah did a little booty shake. Zander quickly looked away.

"How long will you be gracing us with your presence, Mr. Hunley?" Moriah asked.

"Jason, please. I'll be staying a few weeks."

Moriah's eyes widened and she whistled low. "Guess you'll get a chance to sample my gravy and possibly some of our other wares." She pumped her eyebrows at Trin.

Trin scowled back at her. "Honestly, Moriah. You're too much."

Zander smiled and tried to roll his dough flat. He wouldn't mind sampling some of Trin's wares if that's what Moriah was indicating. Since drying up, he hadn't dated often. A few women he'd met in the triathlon circuit were fun to grab dinner with or maybe even share a kiss, but he never went farther than that. He wasn't sure why, but he felt like he needed to figure himself out before he let himself fall for a woman. Sometimes he could swear he felt his mom's influence from heaven. He knew he wouldn't have been able to overcome the alcohol without his guardian angel. Sometimes faith was hard, but a lot of times it was all he had.

"I'll show you too much." Moriah picked up a dish towel and snapped it at Trin.

"Stop!" Trin cried out, holding out a hand to ward her off.

Zander watched them interact and couldn't ignore the rush of jealousy. When he was a boy, he'd loved to hang out in the kitchen with their cook, Hannah. She'd spoiled him with treats and love, but if he ever did anything slightly inappropriate, especially as a teenager when he had a smart-aleck mouth on him and thought it was funny to cuss and shock people, she'd snap him with a dishtowel. It stung. His thoughts pulled around to his mom as they often did. She'd never snapped at him with anything. Even when he'd said curse words, she'd just kindly ask him to please stop. Nothing ever riled that woman and no matter how horrible he acted she thought he was the "best boy". He didn't know if it was a psychological thing she'd done with him or just her natural sweetness. He poked at his still lumpy dough. It didn't matter now.

"It's not getting any flatter doing that." Trin was right next to him.

Zander took a long inhale. She smelled like cinnamon and sugar. He didn't think it was some high-dollar perfume, just her. Sweet and spicy. He liked it.

"Can you help me?" He said in a breathless voice. He knew women loved his deep, husky voice, but he wasn't trying to reel Trin in, she honestly made his voice go all deep and breathy. If it reeled her in, he wouldn't complain.

"Sure." She slid in closer to his side and placed her hands over his on the rolling pin.

Zander smiled to himself. Her slightly calloused hands were still soft and womanly. She could touch him like that all day long.

"The trick is to put some muscle into it." She pressed down on his hands and guided the rolling pin along the dough.

"Oh? I can do that." He inched a little bit closer.

She gave a little sigh and her lips parted. Zander's tongue darted out over his own lips.

"I should hope so with all those muscles," Moriah drawled out.

Zander's head popped up in surprise. He'd forgotten he and Trin weren't alone.

Moriah giggled. "Don't mind me. Just making some cinnamon rolls over here."

"So are we," Trin shot back.

"Whatever helps you sleep at night, girl."

Zander laughed. "You two are like sisters."

"Do you have any sisters?" Trin asked, glancing up at him from beneath thick eyelashes.

"Only child." He kept rolling the dough with Trin's hands over his, ignoring the look the two girls shared.

The dough got flat much too quickly and Trin stepped away from him. He felt the loss immediately. Was there anything else he could think to have her teach him? Something that was hands on. He grinned.

"Now we spread some melted butter on it." Trin whirled away, put a cube of butter in a measuring cup and stuck it in the microwave.

Zander leaned against the counter and watched her. Her legs were long and extremely well-formed. "Did you play a sport in college?"

She whipped around. "Why do you ask?"

He couldn't very well tell her because he was checking out her legs. "I remember hearing that most students at Huntingdon are athletes."

"That's true. Yeah, I played tennis."

"Do you still play?"

"I've been known to."

"Maybe we could have a match. My mom taught me to play a pretty mean game." He hurt at the mention of his mom, even from his own lips, but he kept hoping if he could talk about her casually, some year he might heal from missing her.

"You're on." Trin smirked at him as she returned and spread the butter over his slab of dough.

Zander simply watched her work, liking the smooth muscles in her arms as she moved.

"Now cinnamon and sugar." She produced a shaker and handed it to him.

Zander sprinkled it generously over the dough. "Since this dough is unsanitary, I get to eat all of the cinnamon rolls?"

"What happened to 'I try not to eat sugar' big boy?" Trin teased him.

Moriah laughed. She'd finished her rolls, all perfectly lined up in a pan, and carefully covered them with a clean, white cloth.

"True. You are a bad influence on me. My stomach hurt this afternoon."

She arched her eyebrows. "From half a cookie? Maybe you needed a nudge to the wild side."

"Eating sugar is wild?" Moriah shook her head. "You two's idea of a party is probably ginger ale and snickerdoodles."

"If they're your snickerdoodles." Zander wondered if they knew who he really was, did they also know about his struggle with alcohol? He wouldn't think Moriah would deliberately tease about something so sensitive so maybe she didn't know.

"I'm liking him better and better," Moriah said to Trin.

Zander grinned.

"If you're okay to bake these, I'm going to head out," Moriah continued, taking off her apron and folding it. "I'll be back at five-thirty to start breakfast."

"Thank you." Trin gave the girl a brief hug. "See you bright and early."

"Bye," Moriah said to Zander.

He raised a hand in farewell. She whistled her way out the back door. Zander felt the suddenness of being alone with Trin. He wouldn't complain about it for a second. She glanced shyly up at him then said, "Okay. Now we need to roll them up."

She started at one end and rolled the dough over itself then gestured to him. "It's pretty simple. Do you want to finish it?"

"Sure." He took over and rolled it into a log.

Trin pinched off the edges then demonstrated how to cut the rolls with dental floss and stack them on a cookie sheet.

The silence wasn't awkward, but Zander felt a need to ask, "Does Moriah always work twelve hour days?"

"I try to get her out of here earlier when I can. She's a hard worker and she needs the money." She didn't look at him as she finished lifting rolls onto a cookie sheet and covered them with a thin white towel. She pulled a clean rag from the drawer, got it wet, and started wiping off the counters. "I was going to hire some more help a little bit ago. Moriah does most of the cooking and the housekeeping by herself. I try to help out as much as I can, but sometimes the management responsibilities get crazy." She finished wiping down the counter and turned to face him. "She begged me to let her have the extra hours. It makes me sad she's missing out on time with Turk, but how do I not allow her the chance to provide for herself and her son?"

Zander leaned against the counter. "Where's the father?"

"Who knows? She's definitely not getting any child support."

Zander pursed his lips. "Sad."

"You'd think so, but she comes in here happy as Pollyanna every day." Trin rinsed out the rag and squeezed the excess water out.

"Pollyanna?"

"You never saw *Pollyanna?*"

"Can't say that I've had the pleasure."

Trin laughed. "I don't know that you'd think it was pleasure. It's pretty cheesy, but Pollyanna's parents die and she has to go live with her very stern aunt." Trin pulled a face. "But she always finds something to be positive about and plays some glad game to remember to find the silver lining."

Zander froze as she talked. An orphan who found the silver lining? That definitely wasn't him.

"Like I said." Trin twisted the dishrag between her fingers. "You'd probably think it was cheesy, but Moriah is like that. Always happy. Always laughing and making things fun, even though I know she aches to be with her baby boy and wishes she didn't have to work such long hours to provide for him."

Zander swallowed and grasped for something to say. "Pretty cool that she's willing to work like that. A lot of single moms would probably look for government help or something."

Trin flinched. "Just because people aren't wealthy doesn't mean they're lazy. Usually the exact opposite is true."

Zander felt like it was a personal attack on him. He was wealthy and honestly, pretty lazy. Sure he trained hard for his events, but he didn't do any work that would be considered productive. He'd come up with the ideas for the products for his companies, but he'd paid different teams to invent each one and he had a manager who oversaw everything. Zander didn't have much involvement. The thought of scraping to make ends meet while being a single parent was completely foreign to him.

He looked straight into Trin's deep brown eyes and he read censure there and a little bit of pity. Taking a step back, he said, "Like I said. Moriah is an impressive girl."

Trin sighed and her shoulders sagged. She sat the rag next to the sink. "She's had to grow up quick. Wish I could do more for her, but besides giving her the best pay I reasonably can while still staying within my employee budget, I don't really have any way to change her situation." Trin suddenly looked tired and older.

Zander kept wondering if this was a real *Undercover Boss* what he would and could do to help these people. Buy Trin this house back and let her succeed on her own, have Moriah focus on the cooking and baking, hire someone else to clean, and give Moriah a raise so she could work reasonable hours? He had no clue about Marcus as he didn't really know the guy's story or if he needed help. Maybe he could approach his dad with some ideas. Hopefully he was wrong about his dad planning to sell.

"How old are you?" he asked Trin.

She straightened up and eyed him warily. "Twenty-four. Why?"

"I, um, just interested." Interested in her age or in her? He needed to go for a run or something. Yes, it was a rest day, but sometimes he needed extra movement to help him not want to find the closest convenience store and a nice cold, beer. He could almost feel the cool liquid sliding down his throat. "I'm going to go run around and explore the neighborhood." He had no idea why he thought he had to explain himself to her. That wasn't something he ever did with anybody.

"Have fun. It's beautiful with all the restored homes."

Zander nodded and walked away, knowing she was watching. As he ascended the stairs he felt sad that their interaction had gone from fun and playful to almost sad in such a short time. He hoped he could restore the fun, but he quickly realized how important it was for him to understand their situations. Maybe that was the exact reason his dad had sent him here. He hoped his dad wasn't trying to teach him some humility lesson, but that wasn't really his parenting style. Zander actually felt pretty grateful for this opportunity to look outside himself. It might prove to be as therapeutic as the Tranquility Woods Rehab Center.

CHAPTER 4

Trin woke the next morning feeling groggy and like she might be in the Twilight Zone. She'd stayed up late mulling over everything Zander had said and every look he'd given her. Had she really put her hands over Zander Keller's and helped him make cinnamon rolls? It was too surreal. He was a billionaire heartthrob and she was an average girl who ran a bed and breakfast.

There were things she wasn't excited about either. Why was he here and what did he and his dad have planned? Also, why didn't he have a job or help his dad more? How could a twenty-eight-year-old man be satisfied training for races and not doing much else? It bugged her. Especially when she compared him to someone like Moriah who worked her guts out to try to make her son's life better than hers had been.

Moriah was singing in the kitchen when Trin arrived.

"'And it's a great, daaay to be alive, oh the sun's still shining when I close my eyes. Hard times in the neighborhood, but why can't every day be just this goo-ood?'"

Trin laughed. "If the entire world could be as happy as you in the morning, there would be world peace."

"You know it, girl. No reason not to be happy and praise the Lord. Am I right?"

"You're right, my friend." Trin slipped on an apron and washed her hands. "What are we making to go with the cinnamon rolls?"

"Simple egg and sausage casserole. I'll get it all assembled and in the oven. Why don't you make up the frosting and get those delicious rolls dressed right pretty?"

"I'm on it." Trin pulled out butter, powder sugar, vanilla, and milk. "How's Turk?"

"Oh, that funny little man. He said to me last night, 'Momma, you's my girlfriend.' I laughed so hard I was like, 'Son, I can't be your girl-friend, I'm your momma.' He got that cute little scrunched up face then he grinned and said, 'Otay, I take Twin.'"

Turk couldn't pronounce his r's or k's yet, but he talked really well for a two and half year old. "I'd take him too. What a doll."

"I know it. I am one lucky Momma, I tell you what."

Trin carefully frosted rolls then cut up fruit as Moriah regaled her with more Turk stories, especially about the horrors of potty training a boy. "Then he stinking peed in the garbage can because he couldn't make it to the toilet. Oh, my." Moriah chuckled. "I don't know that I've ever laughed so hard. For a half a second I was mad, I was fuming mad, and then I thought, I can either laugh or I can scold this cute boy and I don't want to be the scolding type. My momma always just laughed and it seemed like the way to go. I did tell him to please try and make the toilet next time."

Trin was laughing so hard her side ached.

"Oh, my," Moriah said a little while later. "It's almost seven."

Trin startled. "Oh! I'll get juice and coffee out then come back for a tray of cinnamon rolls."

"You go, girl. The first casserole just needs to be pulled out of the oven and put in the warming trays."

Trin rushed out into the dining area, hurrying to the arched doorway of the living room to make sure nobody was coming yet and stopped in her tracks. Zander was descending the stairs wearing a t-

31

shirt and running shorts. It wasn't a revealing outfit, but my oh my his calves and biceps were nicely formed. "Good morning," she called out.

"Hey. I'm just headed out on a run. Want to join me?"

She shook her head. "Some of us have to work for a living." She wished she could take the words back immediately as his smile fell and his eyes darkened to a midnight blue.

"Yeah, I guess you do." He studied her with an indiscernible expression and then pushed out the front door and was gone.

Aw, no. She'd just offended him. That wasn't what she wanted to do. Why couldn't she be more like Moriah who loved and accepted everyone? Especially when the one in question was an impossibly handsome rich guy who was probably going to determine her future if he told his dad that she was a brat to a guest and Mr. Keller fired her, or he recommended they sell the house. She needed to turn on the honey not the sass.

Breakfast was moving along slowly but steadily and when Trin heard the front door open, there was no one in the dining room but her. She prayed Zander would come in and talk to her. Listening closely, she could've sworn she heard him pause in the entryway. She wanted to poke her head out the door and say something to him. It might be over the top to officially apologize because then she would be admitting that she knew who he was and that he didn't have a real job. He'd never told her that and he didn't know that she knew who he was. So it would probably be better just to turn on the charm. Seconds later, his footsteps trod heavily up the stairs. Dang.

Mr. and Mrs. Gunnell came down the stairs and into the dining room a few minutes later. An older couple that had visited the Cloverdale every year for as long as Trin could remember, they were like lifelong friends or a surrogate aunt and uncle. They'd loved her grandparents also so that was always a welcome connection.

Mr. Gunnell loved to tease her, especially about finding a billionaire husband. He'd overheard her years ago telling her grandmother about a silly pact she'd made at girl's camp when she was twelve to marry a billionaire. She'd completely lost contact with all the other girls from camp that year. Obviously the billionaire bride pact was nothing more than a pointless pre-teen fantasy, but Mr. Gunnell thought it was hilarious.

Trin started worrying that Zander would come back down when the Gunnells were here. There would be no end to the razzing if Mr. Gunnell noticed how much Zander affected her. Hopefully he wouldn't also piece together that Zander was a billionaire. Yikes.

Footsteps on the stairs came again as she was refilling the apple juice, but to her disappointment, it wasn't Zander. No matter how much teasing she took from Mr. Gunnell, she wanted to see Zander.

One of the honeymooning couples walked in. They'd balked at being called Mr. and Mrs. Nuñes so it was Chad and Kaylee. They were so into each other, they exchanged pleasantries and thanked Trin for the food, but mostly just sat whispering, laughing, or staring into each other's eyes. Trin didn't know if the knot in her gut when she watched them was from jealousy or nausea.

Footsteps came again and Trin knew it was him before she turned and faced the doorway. He was dressed more casually today in a dark grey T-shirt with some kind of pattern on the pocket and fitted khaki pants. She decided the sexy stubble look had been great on him, but clean-shaven was fabulous. Every inch of his face was exactly how a man's face should be—sharp lines, smooth skin, and tan. He obviously spent a lot of time outdoors with his training.

"Is our little Trin going to introduce us to the newcomer or just sit and stare into his eyes?" Mrs. Gunnell asked.

Oh, no. She was getting ribbed by Mrs. Gunnell. Mr. Gunnell must just be biding his time.

"What have we here?" Mr. Gunnell stood and offered his hand to Zander. "Did Trin finally find her billionaire husband and not tell us about him?"

Trin didn't know if she or Zander went more red. Zander at least had the class to shake the man's hand and offer a half-hearted smile.

"No, Mr. Gunnell," she said. "Jason is a guest here. He just checked in last night."

Mr. Gunnell pulled his hand back. "Um, that's a little strange, boy.

33

You don't stay at a bed and breakfast alone. Didn't your mom teach you anything?"

Zander's face pinched at the mention of his mom. Trin's heart went out to him. She knew his mom had been murdered. When she met Mr. Keller for the first time, she'd Googled the family and read the heart-wrenching story.

"I heard Moriah's breakfasts are the best in the south," Zander said. "I figured it was worth being an odd duck who stays alone at a bed and breakfast."

Mr. Gunnell chuckled. "I guess I can't blame you there. You had her biscuits and gravy yet?"

"No, sir."

Mr. Gunnell licked his lips and settled back into his chair, plunging his fork into a bite of egg and sausage casserole. "It's pure heaven, I promise you that."

"I can't wait." Zander shook Mrs. Gunnell's hand and then introduced himself to the honeymooners, who exchanged pleasantries then went right back to feeding each other cinnamon rolls. Gross, but kind of sweet.

Zander came over to the buffet and stood so close to Trin she could smell his very nice cologne. It had to be something expensive to smell perfumed yet manly at the same time.

"I'm sorry about this morning," she blurted out. No! She wasn't supposed to apologize, just change her game plan and be super sweet and accommodating, convince him to tell his dad to give her a raise instead of firing her.

"Sorry for?" He arched an eyebrow at her and the mischievousness in his blue eyes told her he knew exactly why she'd apologized. Did she have to spit it out?

"The me working thing and you not." Oh, that was smooth. She tossed her long hair over her shoulder. "I saved your tray of cinnamon rolls. Would you like me to go get them?"

"Oh, yes, please." He grinned at her, took a clean plate from the stack, and started piling on egg casserole.

"I'll be right back," she murmured. She banged into the kitchen and

Moriah jumped in surprise.

"We low on something?"

"No. Zander's here for breakfast so I'm taking him his cinnamon rolls."

"Ain't that sweet?" Moriah grinned and batted her eyelashes.

"No, it definitely is not sweet. He's too good-looking and too sure of himself and he has that twinkle in those blue eyes. Dang him! I don't know if I want to smack him or kiss him."

"Ooh! He has got you riled up. I like him more every minute."

"That's no way to talk to your boss," Trin threw at her. She took some deep breaths and reached for the plate of cinnamon rolls she'd made specially for Zander.

"You give it to him, sista," Moriah said, laughing as she scrubbed a pan.

"I don't dare," Trin hissed back. "You want me to get us all fired?" She had to play nice to save their jobs and her house.

Moriah's face sobered. "All right, give him the sugar plus a little kiss on the side."

Trin ignored her and pushed back through the swinging door. Zander stood there with an amused smile on his face. Trin blushed and prayed he hadn't overheard her entire conversation. She handed over the rolls.

"Wow. This much sugar might make me sick."

"A little sugar is always good for the soul."

Zander stepped closer, only the cinnamon rolls between them. "What kind of sugar are you referring to?"

Trin swallowed hard. "Um, you know, the regular kind." She wouldn't know how to flirt if she tried. And she probably shouldn't try with her boss's son.

"Oh." He trailed his finger through a bit of extra frosting on the plate and licked it. Trin's eyes widened as she watched his tongue remove the frosting from his finger. He didn't do it all suggestively, more like a little boy tasting the frosting, but there was nothing little about him and she was suddenly short of breath.

"I was hoping for something even sweeter." His blue eyes focused completely on her.

Trin's heart was thumping so hard she was certain he could hear it. What was he doing, bantering with her like this? It didn't help that he was incredibly handsome and she had no clue what role she should be playing. Dutiful employee seemed the best route, but darn it if she could even think straight after watching him lick that frosting. It was such a simple thing, but it seemed incredibly forward and intimate.

"Um, I hope you enjoy your ... sugar." *Cinnamon rolls, not sugar, get it right girl!*

Zander grinned, holding onto the plate, but his eyes roved over her. "I'm sure I will when I get some."

Trin licked her lips, almost panting for air at this point. Moriah had told her to give him the sugar with a little kiss on the side. Her eyes darted to his sculpted lips, no man should have lips that pretty. Not that Zander looked pretty, he was too manly for that. Oh, help. She didn't even try to reply as those beautiful lips smirked at her like they knew exactly how affected she was. Backing away, she half ran to the kitchen. She needed a break from those lips and the penetrating look in his smoky blue eyes before she said more things she shouldn't.

ALONE IN THE DINING ROOM, Zander ate the cinnamon roll slowly. Pretty good for his first attempt at baking. He laughed to himself. The roll was delicious and the uncertain yet interested look in Trin's eyes had been even better. He stared out the windows and felt happier and more at home than he'd felt in ten years. Was it that he was eating sugar and not even feeling guilty about it, or was it the sugar he hoped Trin had been alluding to, that had him feeling grounded and yet excited at the same time?

His phone rang and he glanced at the screen before answering. His dad. "Hello."

"Son. What do you think of the Cloverdale?"

"It's a beautiful home. The restorations you've done are impressive. I feel like I'm living in *Gone with the Wind*." He smiled, thinking of

Trin promising she'd keep Scarlett O'Hara-like harpies away from him.

Glancing around cautiously to be sure he was alone, he stood and walked to the front door, slipping onto the wood-planked porch. It was as perfect as the rest of the house, wide with wood rockers dispersed throughout and white railings. The air had warmed to closer to sixty even though it was barely ten a.m. It was going to be a picturesque fall day in Montgomery.

"Thank you. And the staff?"

There was something in his dad's voice he wished he could get a better read on. What was he playing at? "You realize there are only three of them."

"Is Trin working around the clock?"

"Yes, sir." He smiled to himself. He was picking up the habit too. "And Moriah is working twelve hour days."

"Hmm. I don't like that. Think about a solution for me, son, and then work it out with Trin when she discovers who you are."

"Okay. She probably already knows."

His dad laughed at that. "That's fine. We didn't take any extreme measures to hide it."

Zander gripped the porch railing. "Why did you send me here, Dad? It's miniscule compared to your other properties, and besides them working too much, it seems like everything is running smoothly."

His dad chuckled easily. "Why don't *you* let *me* know that once you figure it out?"

Not the response he wanted. He tried again. "Are you getting ready to sell?" Zander held his breath. The answer would affect Trin immensely and he found himself caring far too much.

"You enjoy your training and keep an eye on things for me. We'll talk in a few weeks. Love you, son."

The phone disconnected and Zander groaned. His dad was being deliberately vague and he knew from long experience trying to pry straight answers out of him when he got like this only resulted in frustration.

Zander turned and caught a glimpse of Trin's brownish-red pony-tail. Had she been spying on him? He smiled at the thought, though he worried that she knew exactly who he was. He'd have to watch her closely and see if he could get the truth out. He smiled. Watching Trin closely wasn't going to be a hard job.

Walking back inside, through the living room and into the dining, he saw her lifting a casserole dish off the side table. She turned to him. "Are you finished with your breakfast, sir?"

So stiff and formal. He hid a smirk. She was obviously trying to act a part. How could he draw her out? "No, I haven't enjoyed my sugar quite long enough." Maybe the sugar innuendo was getting overdone, but he didn't care when her cheeks reddened and she studied the casserole dish.

"I'll leave you to it then." She strode toward the kitchen door.

"Wait." Zander held up a hand and she turned to him. "I'd rather not eat alone. Will you stay with me?"

"I've got to work," she said stiffly.

Ouch. There it was again. Zander wasn't going to be dissuaded though. He liked being around her and Moriah, and his dad had him on assignment, right? He picked up his plate and glass of juice and approached her, stopping close enough he could smell her cinnamon-sugary scent. "You smell like Christmastime." It had been years since he'd paid attention to Christmas smells. Since he refused to go home, his dad would bring Hannah and meet him at one of the resorts where the staff tried their best to make it Christmassy for the family, but the smell was never quite right. Trin's smell was right and then some.

Trin stood like a statue, her chest rising and falling quickly the only indication she wasn't made of stone. Finally, she whispered, "You smell like cologne that somebody spent too much money on."

He should. His Acqua di Parma wasn't cheap and he liked the scent. He really liked that she'd noticed, that he was affecting her.

"If you won't stay with me while I eat, can I come with you?" he asked.

"Where?" Her eyes flickered up to his, wary, yet she couldn't hide that she was interested.

"Anywhere you're going."

Trin laughed, but it wasn't her usual full laugh. "That was cheesy."

"Do you like cheesy?" Unfortunate that he had his plate and cup in his hands or he would've been tempted to touch her right now.

"Usually not." She smiled.

"I like that you can sass me."

"Sass is Moriah's job." She backed into the swinging door. Zander followed, holding it for her with his elbow.

"Hey," Moriah called, scraping uneaten food into the garbage. She glanced up and saw Zander. "Oh! Hey," she drawled the word out. "How were your cinnamon rolls, sir?"

"They were delicious, but not quite as good as the egg casserole."

"Thank you." She gave a bow. "But you didn't finish eating."

Zander walked around Trin and set his plate and cup on the bar, pulling out a barstool. "Trin said I could come eat in here and talk to some beautiful ladies instead of being alone."

Moriah pushed a hand at him. "Oh, Jason, such a schmoozer."

Zander laughed. "That's one I haven't been called before."

"I mean it in the kindest possible way."

Trin set the pan down on the counter. "I didn't say he could come, he followed me." She glanced at Zander before rushing back out to the dining room.

"Ooh." Moriah stacked plates into the dishwasher. "It's pretty early in the morning for you to have already ticked her off."

"I'm not sure what I did." Zander ate another bite of egg casserole, stinging from Trin's hot and cold reception. He usually didn't spend time chasing women. They came to him in droves of their own accord.

"Between you and me." Moriah set a plate in the dishwasher and took a step closer.

The door swung open and Trin entered with the cinnamon roll tray and a carafe of juice. Moriah stepped back and said, "It sure is a beautiful morning. Turk and I are definitely going on a walk to the park after work."

"He'll love that," Trin said.

39

"Where did you come up with Turk?" Zander asked. "My name is unusual so I always like hearing about other unusual names."

"Jason is unusual?" Trin whirled to face him, pinning him with a look.

Oh, no. "Yeah, um, not Jason per se, but Hunley is unusual, and in high school everyone called me by my last name."

"Oh, that makes sense. That you're still keeping a nickname from *high school*." Trin's voice revealed that it definitely didn't make sense. She brushed past him again and back out to the dining room.

"Yikes," Zander muttered.

Moriah quickly darted to his side. "I think she likes you and doesn't know how to deal with it."

Zander reared back, staring at the beautiful young girl. "Really?" He leaned closer. "Why do you think that?"

Trin strode back into the kitchen with her arms loaded with clean cups and plates. She glared at the two of them and muttered, "Bad enough *he* doesn't work."

Moriah arched an eyebrow at Zander and nodded, as if Trin's bitter words confirmed her suspicions. Zander placed a bite of cinnamon roll in his mouth as Moriah went back to loading the dishwasher. So when Trin was interested in a guy she got snippety? That made no sense. Plus, if she knew who he was, like he thought, shouldn't she be buttering up to him to get a raise? He'd think she would worry about the same thing he was worrying about, that his dad was going to sell and she and Moriah would have no guarantees with a new owner.

He watched her unabashedly as she reached up to stack plates in a cupboard. Today she had on tights and a long, blousy shirt. He wouldn't complain about the outfit. Not one bit. She turned and caught him gawking. Zander raised his juice glass to her in salute then took a drink. Moriah burst out laughing and Zander couldn't help the laughter that rose up in him. Unfortunately, his mouth was full of juice, and he sprayed it all over the counter. Moriah's throaty laughter just increased. Trin even cracked a smile, but shook her head at the two of them.

Zander coughed and stood, taking the wet rag Moriah handed to him and swiping up the mess. He looked mournfully at his plate of breakfast that was now cold and soaked in orange juice.

"Oh, heavens!" Trin exclaimed in exasperation. "You're like a little boy that nobody can say no to."

"What?" Zander looked to Moriah for help. She winked at him.

Trin huffed, grabbed a clean plate and filled it with more egg casserole. She plunked it in the microwave.

Zander took the rag to the sink and rinsed it out, handing it back to Moriah with a whispered, "Thanks."

"Sure thing, boss."

Zander's eyes widened. She grinned and scurried away to the broom closet. Trin took the plate from the microwave, added a new cinnamon roll and some fruit then took away Zander's soggy food and refilled his orange juice.

"There," she declared, all but slamming down the cup of juice. "Now stop with the puppy dog eyes."

Zander just stared at her. She was not happy with him today. How grumpy would she be when he wasted that second cinnamon roll? He had to keep that Ironman in his thoughts or he'd be consuming all kinds of Trin-influenced sugar. He was having a hard time thinking of that as a bad thing, liking her sugar and even her sass.

"Um, thanks?" he said.

"You're welcome." She stole the broom from Moriah's hands. "I'll sweep the downstairs." She pushed through the swinging door.

Moriah watched him, nodding her head knowingly. "Um-hmm, my girl is all kinds of affected by you." She snapped her fingers and wiggled her hips. "You got it going on, boy."

Zander chuckled and sat down to his fresh plate of food. He hoped Moriah was right, but he really hoped Trin would start acting as if she liked him, if she truly did. "So, tell me more about your son," he said to Moriah.

She grinned and plied him with funny stories. Zander listened and laughed, but part of his mind was still stuck on all things Trin.

CHAPTER 5

Trin made it through the second day with Zander in residence, mostly trying to avoid him, but he seemed to be everywhere. He and Moriah had formed a quick friendship and she saw him helping Moriah haul bedding and garbage then she caught him chatting with Moriah while she scrubbed down the vacated suite.

Was he interested in Moriah? She wouldn't blame him as Moriah was gorgeous and so much fun to be around, but the girl was much too young for Zander. Couldn't he see that? She huffed. Dang men who liked to rob the cradle.

Finally, he left for a few hours and she felt like she could breathe again. How could one man affect her so much?

The next morning his car pulled out as she was coming into the house at five-thirty to start breakfast. Moriah was already there, forming biscuits for her famous biscuits and gravy. "Good morning, sunshine," she called out.

"Is it?" Trin yawned.

"Every day we get the gift of being alive is a fabulous day, I tell you *what.*" She grinned. "Turk and me had the best time at the park yesterday afternoon. I kept praising the Lord and thinking, 'Why am I so blessed?'"

Trin was suddenly blinking at the wetness behind her eyes. Most people would look at Moriah and notice a single mom struggling to work, raise her son, and find her own independence. She had an apartment over her mother's garage so she had a small measure of privacy, but Trin doubted many outsiders would look at Moriah and think about how overwhelmed she was with blessings.

"Thank you, friend," Trin said. "You always help me put things in perspective."

"Did you see our resident hottie pull out this morning?" Moriah bustled to the stovetop where sausage was sizzling. She stirred and crumbled it as she waited for Trin's response.

"No, I didn't notice."

"Ha! I think you're a liar and you notice everything about that man, including his finely shaped *body*." Of course Moriah couldn't just say it, she had to dance it.

Trin rolled her eyes and grabbed an apron. "I think he likes you."

"Me! I could be his like niece or something. He's too old for me."

"Why did he hang out with you all day yesterday?" Trin couldn't keep the bitterness from her tone.

Moriah chuckled then it turned into her full-blown rich laughter. "Oh, girl, you have got it bad. He's not into me, but you should see the way he watches every move you make and anything I said about you, he'd hang onto with a drip of drool coming out of his fine lips."

Trin washed her hands, shaking her head. She couldn't help but laugh with her friend. "I wish."

"Ha! You admit it. You're into him." Moriah pointed an accusing finger her way.

Trin took over forming biscuits so Moriah could focus on her gravy. "Maybe. He's definitely the best-looking man I've ever seen and he's a nice guy, but he bugs me a little bit too."

Moriah whistled. "Bugging you is good. They got to get under your skin a little bit or they ain't any fun. Am I right or am I right?"

Trin just laughed again.

The morning flew by and she noticed through the window when Zander's Audi pulled back in. Not that she'd been looking out the window all morning, well, she still did her work at least. A little bit later, he came striding into the dining room, where she was restocking the fruit platter. Luckily she was all alone. He looked to be fresh out of the shower and smelled so nice he overpowered the sausage gravy smell.

He took a plate and gave Trin a devastating smile. "Good morning."

"Um, uh-huh. Looks good, yeah." Wow. That was pathetic and too easy to read that she was dying over how good he looked.

"I get to sample the famous biscuits and gravy my third day here? Lucky."

"Yes, you are very lucky. Moriah's biscuits and gravy are *delicious*." Trin could have smacked herself. Why had she emphasized delicious like that? As if she thought he was delicious. Was she as transparent as she feared?

Zander leaned closer and that hot man scent made her want to wrap her arms around his neck. She'd heard about expensive colognes that had pheromones in them to make a woman desire a man. That must be it. It wasn't him. It was his tricky, pricey cologne.

"I'm lucky because I get to see you."

Trin licked at her very dry lips and searched his blue eyes. He looked serious and much too tempting.

"Thank you," she squeaked out.

Zander set his plate down, reached out and took Trin's hand in his own. "I'd love to spend some time with you today."

Trin's throat was dry and her hand was trembling from his warm touch. "I'm very busy today," she sputtered out.

"Let me know if you can fit me in." He squeezed her hand then let it go, giving her one more tempting smile. His blue eyes were brighter today as they twinkled at her like he knew all her most intimate secrets. Darn him all the way to Hades and back.

"Okay." Trin backed away then spun and pushed through the swinging door. "Ooh, that man," she said to Moriah. "Zander is making me crazy! I honestly don't know if I should kiss him or smack him. What? I said the same thing yesterday, didn't I?"

Moriah's eyes had widened throughout Trin's rant. "Uh, girl, you might want to?" She pointed behind Trin.

Trin didn't even need to turn around. "He's right behind me?" she whispered, her heart seeming to stop beating completely.

"He followed you into the kitchen."

Trin clenched her hands and took a slow breath. Now that she had calmed down enough to experience a whole different kind of emotion, namely panic, she could smell him, and she could hear his soft exhalations behind her. She turned slowly and if his eyes had been amused before they were having a stinking party now.

"I'd suggest kissing me. I don't really like being smacked."

"Oh, yeah?" *How dare he?* "Well, maybe I like to smack men who just ... unsettle me."

He chuckled, reached up, and brushed a lock of hair over her shoulder. His fingers lingered on the sensitive skin of her neck and darn it if she didn't tremble and get all weak like one of those wussy girls who had tried to snag Zander on *The Bachelor*.

"I'm sorry if I unsettle you."

"You should be," she flung back at him.

He tilted his head to the side and studied her. "Did you call me Zander?"

Oh, no. She had. The secret was out and he knew that she knew. She was relieved and even more upset at him.

"Yes, I did. You think you're so funny, huh? Trying to trick me. Well I knew from the second you walked in the door. You can't hide a face like that with longer hair and a few highlights." She jabbed a finger at him.

Zander's eyes twinkled at her and she got even more irate.

"I don't know why you're here or what you're playing at, but I am not one of your little flings. If your dad has an issue with how I run my house tell him to come talk to me. I am done dealing with you."

His eyes had gone from amused to wary to angry during her tirade.

She stomped around him, grabbed the plate of cinnamon rolls that he'd made and hadn't finished yesterday and shoved them at him. "Here. I hope the *sugar* makes you sick."

Zander gripped the plate and simply stared at her.

"Girl, what are you doing?" Moriah asked, a note of desperation in her voice.

"I'm sorry," Trin muttered to her friend and she was sorry, but not to Zander. She was sorry that she might have just gotten them both fired.

She hurried to the back door and slipped outside. Running to the swing, she sat in it and let the tears of frustration course down her cheeks. What had she done? Yes, she was angry at Zander, but mostly at herself for being so attracted to him and allowing him to get under her skin. He also was her boss, sort of, and had the power to fire her right now. That thought was terrifying. This house was her entire life. What would she do if she didn't have this connection to her grandparents. To a solid family feeling.

Poor Moriah. What would her friend do if the house was sold or Trin was fired? A smart manager would keep her on because she was an amazing cook, a hard worker, and always positive, but who knew what a different owner would choose to do.

She twisted, grasping the scratchy ropes in her palms. The swing moved slightly. She tipped back her head and stared into the towering oak tree. "What do I do, Nana?" It had been a while since she'd chatted with her grandmother. Not that Nana answered, but sometimes it made her feel better.

"Maybe you give the guy a chance to explain before you rip his head off."

Trin scrambled off the swing and whirled to face him. Explain? No, she definitely hadn't thought of that during her attack on the man. "I, um … please don't fire Moriah."

Zander's serious expression broke and he smiled at her. "Thank you for thinking of Moriah first. Was her Pollyanna story all true or did you exaggerate it?"

"Oh!" Trin fired up again. "Why would I lie to you?"

He shrugged. "Play on my sympathies. You knew who I was and

you're obviously worried about why I'm here. Though I wouldn't recommend screaming at me as the best way to make sure you keep your job."

Trin clenched her fists tight. "I apologize for screaming at you, but I have no desire to 'play on your sympathies.'"

"I'm obviously upsetting you and that isn't why I'm here." He took a cautious step closer.

"Why are you here?" Trin clung to the rope of the swing for stability, but it wasn't much help.

His eyes grew wary again. "I'm not really sure. My dad asked me to do an *Undercover Boss* of sorts."

Trin's breath popped out she exhaled so quickly. Mr. Keller was concerned and had sent his son to figure out the situation. Why? Things were great. Well, they had been until Zander showed up. "Do you think he wants to sell or get rid of me?"

"I don't know." He shook his head. "If it's any consolation I think you're doing a fabulous job."

She bit at her cheek. "Thanks." Was he really on her side? "So you'll give your dad a good recommendation for us?"

"I will. I already have, but he didn't confide his plans, even when I asked him point blank. He's kind of secretive sometimes and it's not like I really work for him. I only help out when he asks me to."

"That's pretty pathetic, you know that, right?" Trin should clap a hand over her mouth, but he really ticked her off. Was he lying when he said Mr. Keller was being vague or was that just his excuse so he could keep observing Trin and driving her nuts?

"Excuse me?"

"You have the chance to work with your dad. To use all that money to make a difference and you … train for Ironmans."

He took a step back. His blue eyes turned a frosty color. "Most people find my dedication to training impressive."

She swallowed hard. Offending him again wasn't the smartest path with everything so unstable. *Think of Moriah, think of your house.* "I'm sure they do. Excuse me. I need to get back to work."

He didn't say anything.

Trin plodded back to the house. She may have just jeopardized hers, Moriah's, and Marcus' futures. She should go back, drop to her knees in front of Zander, and beg his forgiveness. Instead she kept her back ramrod straight and walked away from him. Humility had never been her strong suit.

CHAPTER 6

Zander could understand why Trin would be defensive and testy about him coming here under an assumed name. He could understand that she was concerned about his and his dad's motives and if she was going to lose her job, or the house was going to be sold. What he couldn't understand was how she thought she had the right to basically say he was a worthless member of society because he was pursuing an athlete's path instead of working at a desk job, especially when he didn't need the money. It was his life, not hers. She had no clue how hard he'd worked for the title of recovering addict and to put his mom's death behind him. Exercise was the only way he could clear his mind and keep strong when the desire to quench his thirst overwhelmed him.

He was so angry after their interaction he didn't go back in and eat the breakfast that had smelled so tempting. Instead, he grabbed a Luna bar, filled up his water bottles in his room, and took off on his bike. The ride helped, a little bit.

When he came back, she was in the entryway, checking in a young couple. She gave him a wary smile, which he didn't return. She thought she had the right to righteous anger, well, so did he.

The next few days were tense, to say the least. He kept to himself and focused on his training. He didn't eat their breakfasts, which was definitely better for his training, or say much to anyone. His father had said to observe for a few weeks then get back to him. At this point Zander had no clue what he'd recommend. Yes, he felt sympathy for Trin and Moriah, but Trin needed to make a huge apology to him if she wanted him to be her advocate to keep the house. If selling was even in his father's plan. Ugh. It was all frustrating and he didn't like to deal with problems, it put him on edge.

Because his lame cover was blown, he went and found a stylist to cut the highlights out of his hair. It was nice having it short and normal-looking again. He wondered if Trin liked it short or long then cussed himself for caring what she'd think.

His run Friday morning was on the chilly side. He didn't wear gloves and after an eighteen miler, his fingers were numb and stiff. He plodded up the steps to the bed and breakfast, relieved to be back. Maybe he'd let himself eat one of those breakfasts that he could smell every morning. Moriah was definitely a good cook, if his nose was any indicator. This food wasn't on his training diet, but sometimes he wondered why he cared so much. Trin was right in a way. He was competing in elite athletic events, but who cared what his time or finishing place was. He wasn't winning the Olympics or racing to raise awareness for some social issue. He didn't need to run for a charity, his dad gave huge sums to different charities every year.

He was participating only for himself. Yet, he could easily justify that he needed his exercise schedule to keep strong and build himself physically and emotionally after years of drenching his sorrows in vodka and weed. Luckily, he'd never gotten into anything stronger than that. Sometimes he missed mixing alcohol and marijuana and being "twisted". It would be nice to not deal with issues. He shook his head. No. He couldn't let himself even think about those sensations.

The etched glass door to the bed and breakfast eased open a few inches. Zander felt like the house was welcoming him in, like an old friend who'd been watching and waiting for him. He shook his head. That was crazy thinking. It was simply someone coming out the door with their hands full.

Zander caught the door and pulled it all the way open. Trin was there, struggling with several bags of garbage. She looked gorgeous with her deep red hair pulled into a ponytail, the smooth lines of her neck revealed. Dressed in a teal t-shirt and yoga pants, he couldn't help but admire her lean shape.

"Oh, hey," she said, a bit breathlessly. Was it from hauling the garbage or seeing him? Probably hauling the garbage, she obviously didn't like him.

"Hey."

"How was your run?"

"Cold, thank you."

She gave him a brief smile. Before he could stop himself, Zander stole two of the garbage sacks from her.

"Oh, I've got those," she protested.

"It's no problem." He gestured for her to go in front of him. She led the way down the stairs and around the side of the house to the dumpsters. "Are you helping Moriah clean today?"

"Turk and her mom both have the flu so I told her to take the day off."

"Oh."

Things were so stiff between them. He didn't know how to make it better or honestly if he even wanted to. She still owed him a pretty big apology. They reached the dumpster and he lifted the lid, waited for her to throw in her sack, then tossed his in.

"Thanks," Trin muttered. She turned to face him, folded her arms across her chest, and sighed. "I'm sorry, okay," she flung out.

"Are you really sorry or do you just want me to not fire you?"

Her eyes flashed at him, the dark depths sparking and he could sense she wanted to tell him off again. It made him laugh. The laughter just bubbled out of him and he could see her shoulders relax and then she started laughing too. The laughter felt so good after the coldness and frustration of the last few days. He was reminded quickly of why he'd enjoyed being around her so much.

She finally sobered and bit at her lip. Man, that was a sexy move.

Her lips had been in his daydreams as he ran and rode for miles, even though he wasn't happy with her.

"Is a little of both an acceptable answer?" she asked.

"Maybe." He glanced away from her beautiful face and muttered, "I've never had anybody tell me that what I was doing wasn't good enough. It ticked me off." He focused back on her and surprise was the only way he could think to describe her face now.

"Surely you've had other people in your life who think you aren't living up to your potential."

He shook his head. "Well, our cook, Hannah, would cuss me sometimes if I said a swear word or gave teenage attitude, but my parents … I was an only child and they always treated me like gold. Then after my mom died." He stopped. Had he really just brought his mom up? He rarely did that and this was twice around Trin. He cleared his throat and continued, "I've never gotten close enough to anyone to have them be so honest with me." Even when he had gone through addiction recovery, the high-dollar facility was all about positive reinforcement and nobody had ever told him he was a waste of space like he assumed Trin wanted to tell him.

"Wow." She pursed her lips. "I'm sorry you don't have anyone close and …" She dipped her head. "And about your mom. You've gone through hard things, my friend."

Zander's entire body warmed at those words, my friend. He hadn't had a real friend in … he couldn't even remember how long. "Are we?"

"What?" She cocked her head to the side and her long, silky-looking hair caressed her shoulder. Zander wanted to run his fingers over her hair and her shoulder. He wasn't sure which first.

"Friends?" He asked softly.

Trin studied him. "You're lonely."

Zander took a step back. "Whoa."

"Sorry." She heaved a deep breath. "I really am sorry. That's not my place."

She was right it wasn't her place, but she was more right that he was lonely. Very. He'd distanced himself from everyone, even his father. He was a loner in every sense of the word and honestly, it was about as much fun as working to stay sober. No wonder being around Trin and Moriah, smiling and laughing, had been the happiest he'd been in a long time.

"It's okay," he said quickly. "If we're going to be friends I guess you can say things like that."

She smiled and he had never been so drawn to a woman. How could a smile be that irresistible and just downright adorable? He smiled. Not sure if the word adorable had earned a spot in his vocabulary before today.

"Friends?" She stuck her hand out.

"Friends." Zander grasped her much smaller hand and shook it.

"I'll catch you later, friend." Trin winked and his heart rate increased. "I'd better get back in there and make sure nobody's needing anything else for breakfast. It's going to be a long day without Moriah. Luckily no one is checking out, so there's just the light cleaning."

"I'll help you." The words were out before he could stop them, but he realized he didn't want to take them back. He could learn a lot from spending the day working with her. The thought of spending an entire day getting to know her better didn't hurt either.

Her eyes widened. "What?"

"I'm supposed to be doing this *Undercover Boss* thing and that's obviously failed with my lame disguise." He pointed to his short, dark hair. "If I help you do your work today then I'll have more to report to my dad."

"Let me get this straight. The ultra-wealthy, ultra-handsome, ultra-athlete wants to do dishes, freshen up towels, and wipe up toothpaste spills?"

"You think I'm ultra-handsome?"

"Don't let it go to your head." She blushed and started to walk away.

Zander caught up to her. "I'll try not to."

She laughed.

"So, what's on the schedule first?"

"I can't get you dirty."

53

"I just got back from an eighteen-mile run. I don't think a little dirt is going to hurt this sweaty body."

"Wow. Eighteen miles. I can't go that far in my car without stopping for a Coke."

He chuckled. "You're in better shape than you think. I bet you could keep up."

"With you? Not a chance."

Zander tamped down the surge of pride her answer gave him. She realized what an elite athlete he was, even if she thought it was a lame career for an adult.

They reached the steps and ascended to the front porch. "You really want to help?" she asked, still sounding doubtful about his ability to work.

"Yes, please." He'd never done a day of labor in his life. As a child, he'd help out around the house and his parents thought it was so cute when they caught him working with the gardener, Mr. Tyler, or in the kitchen with Hannah, who was more like a beloved aunt than an employee, but it was really all for fun. Wiping up toothpaste? Definitely not. But it couldn't be any harder than running a marathon.

"Don't you need to eat something first? Refuel from your run?"

"Yeah, I probably should. I drank a Reliv 24K when I finished, but some real food always helps."

"I don't even know what language you were speaking on the twenty-four thing, but you eat then you can come help me in the kitchen if you're really sure that's what you want to do."

"Sounds good." He wanted to be with her. Even though she was probably too honest with him. He liked her and the way she made him smile. If that meant unfamiliar manual labor. Bring it on.

Trin watched Zander fill his plate and joke around with the Thompsons, one of the honeymooning couples, as he started to eat. It was ten o'clock, but she wanted to leave the food a little longer in case Zander wanted seconds. He'd just run eighteen miles? Insanity. He pushed himself physically yet he openly admitted that he'd never been put in his place and she highly doubted he knew what manual labor even was. After they finished with the kitchen and cleaning rooms, she would have him go out on the grounds with her and trim some dogwood bushes that were getting out of control by the back fence. Hopefully there were a few weeds in the garden to pull as well. This was going to be fun.

She loaded the dishwasher and then went back out to the dining room to start clearing the food. Zander saw her and jumped to his feet. The Thompsons had finished and disappeared. He stacked the plates on the table into a pile and followed her back through the swinging door. They worked in near silence, except for him asking occasionally where she wanted something put as they cleared the dining room and wiped it down then he finished loading the dishwasher while she put food in containers.

"This thing is full," Zander said. He tried to push it closed, but he'd stacked the bottom rack too high and one of the pans hit into the top rack.

Trin smiled and pulled the pan out, setting it in the sink. "Let's run this load then we'll do another load later with the bigger pans."

"Okay. So we're done in here?"

Trin nodded, putting detergent in and starting the dishwasher. "You're doing pretty good so far, Mr. Bachelor."

Zander groaned. "Please don't say you watched that show."

"I think every single woman in America watched that show."

"I'm not sure if that's a compliment to me or not. Did you watch it because I was so good-looking you couldn't pull your eyes away or so pathetic you wanted to fix me? Because I swear every woman on there wanted to fix me."

"I thought you said I was the first person to ever call you out."

Zander leaned against the counter and Trin had to wonder if a man leaning like that had ever affected her so strongly. He just had the leaning thing down. "In that way, yes you were. You should feel special."

She blushed. For some reason she felt very special with him looking at her like that.

Zander smiled at her then he looked down and continued, "The women wanted to help me get over my mother's death, and I'm sure they wanted to help me stop being a drunk. But they never called me out, it was always this super sweet, if you love me I can cure all your ills type of thing."

"But none of them were worthy of your love?"

He shifted his weight. "It wasn't them. Despite what the show encourages, there were some really nice girls. I just wasn't in a great place, probably the lowest time of my life. It was shortly after that I admitted myself to Tranquility Woods and started my recovery. Embarrassing to think I was on national television high or wasted most of the time."

Trin appreciated that he would share this with her, especially after how she'd treated him. "You did a pretty good job of covering it up. I wouldn't have thought you were drunk."

"That's good to know. Probably more the producers did a good job of covering it up. It makes me wonder though ..."

"What's that?"

"All those women, some of them were such harpies."

"Scarlett O'Hara?" Trin smiled.

"Exactly. Scary Scarlett. But a lot of them were nice girls and I couldn't understand. Did they just want to win for the sake of winning? Why would they compete for someone like me? Who would want to saddle themselves with an addict, no matter how wealthy he was."

Trin thought he was selling himself short. He may have been an addict, but he had treated the women on the show really well and he wasn't just insanely wealthy he was insanely handsome. It was a hard combination for a lot of women to resist. "For somebody who's never heard a negative word in his life, you're awfully down on yourself," she tried to joke to lighten the mood.

He shrugged. "Just being truthful. I look back at myself then and I wouldn't want to be around me."

"You went through some tough times, but it looks like you've come out stronger on the other side."

"You'd like to think so." He pushed away from the counter. "We've got work to do. What next?"

She smiled. "You're a gungho worker, now?"

"Hey. One day in a lifetime, should be fun, right?"

Trin thought she shouldn't comment on that one. She led the way to the laundry room. The cleaning cart was already stacked with fresh linens and supplies. She'd done this most days of the week for she couldn't remember how long. The novelty of cleaning rooms back when she'd followed her nana around had definitely worn off, but there was still satisfaction in a job well done and their guests were usually respectful and didn't leave disgusting messes, thank heavens.

Zander took the cart and pushed it to the elevator that had been installed in a renovation before Trin's time, in the spot where the dumb waiter used to be off the kitchen. It was a little awkward when a guest needed the elevator, as they had to bring them through the kitchen, but it met code, and wasn't used often for guests as there were four guest suites on the main level past Trin's office, so anyone who needed accommodations without stairs was booked into one of those rooms.

They rode up to the second floor then started, ironically, with his room, which was at the far end of the hall.

"This is a little awkward, you coming into my room like this," Zander said. "We're just friends, remember, no pushing things to the next level."

"Oh, don't you wish."

"You have no idea."

Trin laughed and had to look away from the smolder in his blue eyes.

He'd already made his bed so they didn't have to do anything there. "I'm impressed the rich boy made his bed."

"There's a lot you don't know about me, girl." He imitated Moriah's nickname.

"I'm seeing that." His room had been in good condition every time she'd cleaned it instead of Moriah.

She showed him how to switch out towels, breathing deeply of the rich cologne that she'd come to identify him with. She saw a yellow bottle on the counter that read, Acqua di Parma. "Is that the cologne you wear?"

"Yeah."

"I like it." She more than liked it, she would inhale it all day if she could, especially if he was wearing it.

"Thanks. I should have some on right now. I hope I don't stink like sweat."

"You don't. You kind of smell ... salty."

He pumped his eyebrows. "I taste salty too."

Oh, my. She did not need to be thinking about how he tasted as she stood in his bathroom and smelled his cologne and felt completely surrounded by his presence. "Um, do you want more shampoo, conditioner, or lotion?"

"No, thanks. I have my own shampoo and I don't use conditioner or lotion."

"Gotcha." Snapping gloves on, she grabbed his garbage liner out and replaced it with a new one, tossing it into the trash on the cart. She sprayed the counter and wiped it quickly with a paper towel.

"I thought I was supposed to be doing this," he protested.

"Watch and learn. I'll let you take Mr. and Mrs. Gunnell's room. One of them smears toothpaste all over the place."

"Okay. I'll be ready." He smirked and did that stinking leaning thing, this time against the wall as she tried to concentrate on wiping his counter clean.

Glancing around the room, she took one more deep breath of his cologne and gestured to the door. "I think we're good here."

"Looks great." He followed her out of the room with the cart.

The other rooms went quickly and she only teased him a little bit when he couldn't figure out how to squirt the spray bottle that was turned to off and didn't know that he needed to knot the garbage liners to make sure they stayed properly in place. Otherwise the liner would collapse into the small garbage cans and she'd be fishing someone's disgusting garbage out later.

As they exited the last room, she turned to him. "Thanks for your help. It was fun."

"It was. Anything else you need help with?"

She studied him. Did he really want to keep working with her? She liked being around him. Could it be possible he was feeling the same? "I have a few things I was going to do on the grounds then mostly just paperwork this afternoon."

"Why don't I help you on the grounds then grab a shower. After that, would you mind showing me the profit and loss statements?"

"So you do know a little bit about running a business?"

"Hey, I graduated from NYU in business. Just because I did it with a lot of help from Jack Daniels doesn't mean I didn't learn anything."

"I'll take your word for that."

They reentered the elevator. "You're really open about your alcohol addiction."

He pushed the button and turned to face her. "Only with you actually. I don't like to talk about it much."

She couldn't believe this man, who was so easy to be around, wasn't close to anyone. How sad. "Now I feel really special."

"You should. Cause we're friends, right?"

"Yes, friends."

He gave her this look that was way past friends and just about made her melt into a puddle. He was sweaty and still in running clothes and she probably smelled like plastic cleaning gloves and disinfectant, but still she was tempted to hit the button to stop the elevator and see if she should kiss him like he'd suggested a few days ago.

The elevator dinged and the doors slid open, yanking her back to reality. Zander broke her gaze and pushed the cart out. She led the way into the laundry room and showed him how to load and start the washing machine.

"I can't believe you've never done laundry in your life."

Zander shrugged. "Loser, eh?"

"You're pretty far from a loser. It's just ... such a different lifestyle than I can understand."

"We all have our own realities, I guess."

She guessed he was right, but honestly. To be twenty-eight years old and not know how to run a washing machine? They went outside and found Marcus raking leaves. He lifted a hand in greeting. Trin waved then led Zander to the back of the property and opened a shed. "I need to trim some bushes. I guess you've probably never done that either."

"Actually, I have. I used to love helping the gardener back home. He was this cool old guy, Mr. Tyler. He passed away a couple years ago." Zander suddenly blinked and looked away.

Trin laid a hand on his arm. "You okay?"

He nodded. "I just feel bad that I didn't say goodbye to him."

"You haven't been home in a while?"

"Ten years."

Trin's eyes widened. She didn't even like her stepdad and she was really busy running this place, but she still tried to go home at least once a year. Mr. Keller encouraged her to block out weeks with no reservations so she could take a true vacation and he could bring in crews to do updates. She'd taken a couple weeks last summer when it was hot and miserable in Montgomery. She didn't go home the entire time, but she did go see her family. Her mom and half-brothers and sisters were always fun to be around.

"So, which bushes?" Zander clutched the trimmers.

"Over here." She grabbed her own pair and walked to the border of the property on the west side. "We just need to trim them so they look more orderly, less out of control."

"Okay." Zander set to work and soon they had a sizeable pile of branches. "Not that I mind doing this, but isn't it Marcus' job?"

"I should make him do it, but he's pretty busy with other projects. He fixes stuff all the time. Even though we've done a lot of renovations to the place it's still a hundred and fifty year old house. I honestly make a daily list of little things for him to fix. He saves us a ton of money because we don't have to bring specialized workers in all the time."

"That's good. So, what's his story?"

"I don't know a whole lot about him. He asked me for money down on the Riverwalk almost a year ago now. I gave him a couple of bucks and told him he could have a job if he cleaned up."

"That was brave."

"I guess. I know how it is to be alone." Why did she admit that to him? She might as well spill all, that after her grandparents died she really felt like she was on her own. "I wanted to help him," she said quickly.

"Has he cleaned up?"

Trin shrugged. "He doesn't work plastered, but I've seen a lot of beer cans in the garbage."

Zander looked sharply at her. "Don't you both live in the guesthouse?"

"Yes."

"Do you think that's smart?"

Trin bristled. "I can take care of myself."

"I'm sure you can, but you don't understand the strength and lack of brainpower of someone that's intoxicated."

"Spoken like someone who's been there."

"I have." He clipped more vigorously. "Luckily, I never hurt anyone while under the influence, but I know some who have."

Trin sighed. "I lock my door at night. Don't worry."

"I will worry."

"Why?" She stopped clipping and turned to face him.

"Because we're friends." Zander beseeched her with those smoky blue eyes and she probably would've agreed to anything he said at the moment. "Please watch yourself and don't be alone with him outside of work."

"Okay," she whispered.

"Maybe I can find a way to help him."

Trin didn't know what to say, but appreciated that he cared. The branches were snipped and cleaned up quickly and there weren't enough weeds in her garden to keep them busy nearly long enough.

"I think I'll change out of my work clothes and do the paperwork. You wanted to shower?"

"Yes, ma'am."

Trin smiled. "You may have proven yourself a decent worker, but you don't get to yes ma'am me."

"Forgive me?" He brushed the hair from her neck, his fingers grazing the sensitive skin.

"Sure." Trin moved a few inches closer, mesmerized by his smoky blue eyes.

The roar of a motor pulled them apart. Marcus blew leaves out from underneath the trees' branches and was headed their direction. Trin turned and walked back to the house. Her time with Zander had left her liking him a lot more. If she wasn't careful, she was going to kiss her boss and complicate her life far too much.

CHAPTER 7

Zander was impressed with Trin in more ways than he could count, but terrified of her naivety around Marcus and the way she made Zander feel. He participated in Ironmans because they exacted everything from him and made him feel accomplished and alive. Trin could make him feel more alive than he ever had just by a simple look or a touch of her hand on his arm. The past couple of days, he'd spent more time with her than he had on his training. His training had taken precedence, almost from the day he walked out of Tranquility Woods. To be more focused on a woman than his next race was an odd switch for him.

He'd tried to talk to Marcus about getting help, but the kid had almost growled at him and brushed him off. Maybe Marcus was just a social drinker, but something about him didn't bode well with Zander. He wished he could help the kid get admitted to somewhere and get help, but the person had to be willing to get treatment, unless it was court-ordered.

Part of him knew he needed to slow down where Trin was concerned, but he wasn't listening to that voice as he picked up drunken noodles, curry, pad Thai, basil rolls, and chicken skewers from the Green Papaya. He'd rarely seen Trin take time off and he probably couldn't talk her into letting Marcus man the bed and break-fast after Moriah went home so Trin could take a break. How did she ever get a vacation? She worked night and day. He needed to talk to his dad about that one too. He hoped she was making a lot of money, giving her life to her job and this house like she did. The house was like her family. He couldn't even imagine what she'd do if his dad sold it or changed management. Zander would fight his dad if he tried.

He drove into the bed and breakfast and parked his rented Audi in one of the guest spots. Whistling as he took the food up the walk, he wondered how to kidnap her for a semi-date. She was sitting at the front desk, tapping away on the computer with her ear to the phone. "Thank you, Mr. Finley. I've got your reservation down for January fourth through the ninth. We look forward to seeing you." She set the phone down and her eyes met Zander's. Her smile seemed to pene-trate into his soul.

He held the food aloft. "Hungry?"

"Yes. How did you know?"

"I'm finding that you work far too much and don't take near enough time for yourself."

"You could kidnap me and take me to Tahiti."

He thought that was the best idea he'd ever heard, but couldn't believe she'd made the suggestion. He'd enjoyed his last trip to Tahiti. He'd never traveled with someone before. With Trin, he could imagine all kinds of possibilities that had his neck burning.

"I sure could," he said, "but you'd probably have a panic attack worrying about deserting Moriah and your house."

She sighed. "You're right." She stood and they walked to the kitchen.

"Why don't you hire more help? At least a night manager and an assistant housekeeper. You shouldn't be doing so much and neither should Moriah."

They settled into barstools at the wide counter and Zander started pulling containers out of the sacks. It was comfortable and familiar, like he picked up takeout for them often instead of this being the first time.

"Moriah needs the money and I, well ..." She opened the container of basil rolls. "Oh, yum. Thank you. Who told you that I love Thai food?"

"Lucky guess."

"Moriah. Right?"

He grinned, but wasn't revealing his source. He'd quizzed Moriah this morning when she was restocking linens after he came back from a long swim at the local YMCA.

"You were going to tell me why you haven't hired more help?" He prodded, opening the container of drunken noodles and grabbing some with his chopsticks.

She chewed slowly on a basil roll. "I love that we're just eating straight from the containers."

He loved it too, it felt very intimate. "You're dodging my question."

"Okay." She stood and got them each a glass of ice water. "The truth is that I don't have anything else to do, anywhere else to be. I'm a pathetic loser. There." She slammed his glass of water down in front of him and scowled. "You happy?"

"Thank you for the drink." He smiled and waited until she sat down and took a chicken skewer before saying, "We have a lot in common, don't we?"

"We have absolutely nothing in common. You're an entitled rich kid and I'm a worker bee."

Zander didn't let that offend him. She lashed out when cornered. "We're both trying to find our place in life and are basically alone. You have this place, and I have my training."

Trin set the skewer down on a napkin. Her dark eyes were conflicted. "I have Moriah."

"Yes, you do. You're very lucky to have such a good friend, but what about friends outside of this place?"

She bit her lip and then took a sip of water. Zander tried to give her some space by popping a large bite of curry in his mouth. It was spicy. He ate another bite and felt sweat breaking out on his forehead. "That curry is amazing," he told her.

Trin tried some curry. She immediately grabbed her water glass and downed a large swallow. "Too much for me. Yikes! I'm sweating."

"Me too." Zander laughed. He ate a chicken skewer. They were okay, much better with the creamy peanut sauce. "So? Can I talk to my father about expanding your employee budget so you can hire the help you need?"

"Do you know why he wanted you to come? If he's going to sell?"

"He won't tell me much. Maybe he just wants me here so I can train for my races while I get to know you and Moriah."

Trin looked at him doubtfully.

"You're still dodging the subject," he said. "How are we going to get you to take some time off?"

"It won't matter if my house, I mean, your house, gets sold."

"Let's focus on what we can change," he suggested.

Her eyes flashed at him. "I'll make you a deal."

"Okay." He was suddenly wary.

"I'll look into hiring some more help and taking some breaks if you talk to your dad and make sure he isn't going to sell or fire me."

He could talk to his dad again, though he wasn't sure he'd get a straight answer. Thankfully that was the deal she wanted to make. He was afraid she was going to ask him to go to a psychiatrist to get over his guilt with his mom which was a crazy worry as they hadn't even talked about his mom. Besides her thinking he was lazy for not working, she didn't seem to be concerned with his deep-seated issues. Then he realized it was probably because she wasn't thinking about some long-term relationship. He wasn't sure what he was thinking, besides wanting to be around her every minute.

TRIN DIDN'T KNOW what was happening to her. She was falling for a pretty boy who didn't know how to work. Okay, that wasn't really fair. The past few days he'd worked alongside her and he was actually a quick learner and a hard worker. Obviously, the training he was doing was incredibly tough and he knew how to push himself physically, but why didn't he engage in real life, real relationships? He was almost thirty years old and was basically freeloading off his father. At least, that's what she had thought before, but now she knew that wasn't exactly true. The businesses he'd created selling everything from supplements to clothing to the Ironman circuit were hugely successful. He couldn't have created them without his father's backing, but it was still great that he'd created something.

The things she's learned about him were changing her opinion drastically—he had a successful business, he wanted to help her, he'd committed himself in an effort to be better than an addict and alcoholic, and he was kind. All these things made him irresistible to her. And when he smiled at her or talked to her or touched her. My, oh, my. She didn't care that his background differed vastly from hers and they both had commitment issues, she just wished he would kiss her.

They combined the leftover Thai food and put it away in the fridge. "Thank you for dinner, that was delicious."

"Anytime. Do you always just eat here?"

"Yeah." She watched him warily as they walked back out into the dining room toward the front desk. "Don't think I never get a break. I go run errands when Moriah's here."

"Oh, that's relaxing and fun." He shook his head. "Errands for yourself or for the house?" He eyed her closely.

"Um, both." She didn't really have many errands for herself. She did most of her shopping online. She loved this house, the work, and interacting with the people. The only thing she really missed was playing tennis, and you had to have a partner for that, not just free time.

Mr. Gunnell was in the dining room, loading up on cookies. "Hey. Have you tried these snickerdoodles?"

Zander nodded. "I ate one the first day I got here."

"You could probably use ten more. All muscle and bone. Women like a little something around the waist." Mr. Gunnell winked.

Trin hid a smile. Mr. Gunnell had more than a little around the waist and she thought Zander looked just about perfect.

"So, you're still here," Mr. Gunnell continued. "Pretty odd for a single guy to want to hang out at a honeymooner's spot."

Zander gestured to Trin. "I'm trying to recruit her to the honeymoon idea. Don't ruin my game, man."

Trin looked at Zander, incredulous. He winked and she started laughing. He was teasing. Darn, disappointing, but still pretty funny.

Mr. Gunnell swung to face Trin. "That so? You think you're good enough for our Trin, Mr. Hunley?"

Trin had almost forgotten about the assumed name. That was definitely for the best. If Mr. Gunnell knew who Zander was, he'd either try to force Trin on him or talk his ear off about business. The older gentleman owned a string of dry cleaners.

"No, sir." Zander's gaze swept over her and she quivered from his warm look. "I would never kid myself that I'm good enough for her, but I keep hoping that she'll look past my faults and give me a chance anyway."

Mr. Gunnell nodded thoughtfully and popped another half of a cookie into his mouth. He chewed and swallowed while Zander continued to stare at Trin with those irresistible blue eyes. She involuntarily stepped closer to him. She would give him a chance. What woman wouldn't?

Mr. Gunnell slapped Zander on the shoulder. "That's all we can hope for, son. I tricked my wife into thinking I was rich. Most blessed day of my life when she said yes to me. You marry up and they make you into a better man than you could imagine." He paused. "One important question, though, are you a billionaire?"

"Oh, Mr. Gunnell, no." Trin's face burned with embarrassment. Not now.

"Um." Zander half-laughed. "Yeah, I am." He glanced at Trin. "Does that help?"

"For this girl, it might be important." He grabbed a few more cookies, winked at Trin, and sauntered out of the dining room.

"What was all that about?" Zander asked.

"Oh, my." Trin shook her head. "I made a dumb pact at girl's camp, about a …" She blew out a long breath. "A billionaire thing and Mr.

Gunnell found out about it." Hopefully, that explanation would suffice. Darn her friend, Erin, tricking her into that pact. She rarely thought about it, except when Mr. Gunnell teased her.

Zander studied her. "Since I am a billionaire, would you give me a chance?"

Trin took another step closer. They were inches apart now. "A chance for what?"

Zander cupped her cheek with his hand. She could smell his delicious cologne and her stomach was erupting with butterflies. "To get to know you, to be with you."

This was all moving really fast for Trin and she was still troubled by their differences in lifestyle. She could never leave her house and travel the Ironman circuit with him, but at this precise moment, she couldn't say no to this incredibly handsome man if she'd wanted to. Her body had its own agenda. She ran her hands up his muscular arms to his shoulders and felt him tremble under her touch. He caught a breath and knowing that she affected him like this emboldened Trin. Standing on tiptoes, she pressed her body against his and softly kissed him. Zander froze. He simply stared at her, with his hand still on her cheek. He didn't respond to the kiss or make a move to continue it.

Trin fell back onto her heels, embarrassment washing over her. Zander blinked and exhaled roughly. The moment stretched between them. Trin didn't know if she should apologize for the kiss, back away, or remove her hands from him. She stood there and stared at him.

Zander was much too serious as he ran his hand along her cheek and through her hair. "It's like silk," he muttered.

"Are you okay?" she whispered.

He shook his head. "Do you know how long it's been?"

Okay, this was getting really awkward. "What?" If they were going to compare the last time they kissed someone, she was out.

"Since someone has touched me?" he murmured.

Really, really awkward. "You had women all over you on *The Bach-*

elor. You probably have women all over you everywhere you go." She'd seen photos to prove that.

He shook his head. "No, I mean, yes, those women tried to touch me, but you touch me." He placed a hand over her heart. Her pulse skyrocketed and she knew he could feel how fast he had her heart thumping. Zander cupped her face with both hands and lowered his lips so close she could almost taste the mint he'd popped in after dinner. "I've never let anyone touch me like that," he whispered.

In the next breath he was kissing her and the world completely disappeared. Zander's warm lips commanded every ounce of her attention. Her hands moved from his shoulders to his biceps and she clung to him as he communicated what he'd been trying to tell her. He touched her in a way that she'd never been touched either. It wasn't just physical, even though the physical part was amazing. It was deeper, more meaningful, something you didn't feel with just anyone.

"Ahem." A throat was cleared loudly and they pulled apart, both breathing hard.

"The missus wanted a cup of tea." Mr. Gunnell was clearly enjoying this. "Don't let me interrupt you folks."

Zander chuckled and wrapped his arm around Trin. "Don't mind us." He directed her back through the swinging door into the kitchen. They both started laughing. "I thought Mr. Gunnell had my back, but apparently not."

"I've got your back," Trin said.

His eyebrows arched. "Yeah?" He pulled her close again. "I've got all of you."

"Don't let me go," Trin whispered.

"Not a chance."

His lips descended on hers again and she didn't care about their differences. Most people never found a connection like this in their entire lives.

CHAPTER 8

Zander stumbled as he walked down the hotel hallway. He grinned, remembering the girl who'd been all over him at the bonfire. She hadn't even realized he was only a senior in high school. He looked older and he could hardly wait for college life. The women were going to flock to him when he played football for Auburn University.

He pulled the key card out of his pocket and stared at it for a few seconds. Which way did it go in? How to open the door quietly so he didn't wake his mom? He felt a slight flush of guilt as he pulled his phone out to check the time. Two-thirteen in the morning. Had his mom gone to sleep okay? She was so nice to him, but sometimes he got annoyed with her. Dad had spoiled her too much and without his dad here, Zander felt like he had to be there for his mom every second. He shouldn't feel guilty because he'd gone to a bonfire on a recruiting trip. He hoped his mom was asleep though. She'd be upset if she found out he'd been drinking. Her oldest brother had ruined his liver and died a pathetic alcoholic, with Zander's dad and mom the only ones who took care of him. Now she preached to Zander constantly about how some people were more easily addicted than others. Blah, blah, blah.

He finally got the key card inserted properly, the green light flashed and he pushed down the handle and quietly swung the door open. He shut it behind him, listening for his mom's soft breathing, but there was nothing.

Weird. He flipped on the bathroom light and his world upended. Blood covered the mirror, counter, toilet, and shower. His mom lay on the tile floor, her head tilted at an angle that Zander knew wasn't natural. Her eyes were closed, her clothes were ripped, and blood and cuts covered her once-smooth skin.

Zander screamed and dropped to his knees. He shook her. "Mom! Mom, please!" She was limp in his arms like there was no substance to her anymore. "No, Mom, wake up!"

Sobs worked their way up from his chest and out his throat. He tasted salt and saw his own tears splash onto his mom's hair. He gently laid her back on the cold tile and felt for a pulse, for some sign of life. There were slash marks all over her body. Zander prayed like he'd never prayed in his life, even though he was the last one who had the right to pray. Please, let this be a dream. Don't let it be real. My mom. Not my mom.

He tried to remember CPR, breathing into her mouth then compressing her chest, but there was so much blood everywhere. The salt from her blood mingled with the salt from his tears and he choked down vomit.

He had no clue how much time had passed when he finally admitted that he was too late. She was gone. He leaned against the toilet and pulled her head into his lap and the sobs and tears kept coming as he held her. This was his fault. How could he have left her alone? She needed him and he'd failed her so he could flirt with girls and drink.

He worked his phone out of his pocket, trying not to disturb her head and pressed his dad's number.

"Hello?" his dad's voice was scratchy with sleep.

"Dad!" he screamed into the phone, cradling her head against his stomach. He couldn't let her go. Why had he let her go? "Someone killed her," he moaned out.

"What?"

"Dad," his voice cracked and he had to force out the words. "Someone killed Mom."

"No, no!" His dad let out a scream that wasn't human.

Zander could hear his dad crying like the world had ended and knew that their world had. The weight of his failure crashed down on him. His beautiful mother. Had she suffered? Looking down at her, he knew she had. It was all his fault.

Zander flew upright in bed, screaming like his dad had that night. Sweat poured down his chest. It took a few seconds to remember he was in Montgomery. His mom was still gone. He and his dad were still alone. It was still his fault. He couldn't hold back the sobs. It had been ten years and the nightmare made him bawl every time.

Trin struggled coming out of sleep. When she did, she tried to remember what had awakened her. She could've sworn she heard screaming coming from the main house. She slid into a tank top, shorts, and Sanuks, and crept out her door and across the lawn. It was chilly tonight, but the full moon reflected off the shiny grass and made it so she didn't need any light. She hugged herself for warmth and wondered if she should call 911, but that seemed silly. She didn't even know what she'd heard, just that instinct that something wasn't right and she needed to investigate.

She unlocked the back door with her key and slowly eased into the kitchen. A large shadow was standing next to the open industrial fridge. She screamed and the man whirled to face her. Zander. She placed a hand over her quickly beating heart.

"What are you doing?" she asked.

He swung the fridge closed and stared at her. The moonlight coming through the windows gave enough light to see that his expression was guarded and unsettled. His body was shaking. It wasn't cold in here, but he was only wearing some silky shorts.

"Are you okay?"

He shook his head and looked around the kitchen as if searching for something.

"Zander." She stepped closer to him. Did he sleepwalk or have night terrors? That was how he was acting, like he wasn't quite awake or quite himself. "Was it you who was screaming?"

"Screaming? Me? How do you know?" Zander clenched his hands

together, but she could still see them trembling. He paced back to the white cabinets and opened one, staring inside it blankly.

"Can I help you with something? What do you need?" Trin felt like she was in a scary movie where you weren't sure why someone was acting the way they were.

"Help?" He startled as if he'd forgotten she was there. "I need, um." He paced and bumped into the counter. "Sugar. Maybe sugar can help."

Trin was certain this suggestion of sugar was not any kind of flirtation on his part. She stepped next to him, grasped his elbow, and directed him onto a barstool. He allowed himself to be manipulated like a small child. "Sit. I'll get you some chocolate chip cookies and hot cocoa."

"Hot cocoa? No, I need something stronger." His eyes got a far-off look then he sighed sadly. "Coffee." He swallowed hard and muttered, "Coffee might help."

Trin could see he was deeply disturbed and was ready to slam something much stronger than coffee to help with the pain. "No way. As strung out as you are at the moment, coffee would keep you up all night."

"Won't sleep anyway," he muttered. He stared out the window. The oak tree leaves gently swayed in the breeze, but Trin didn't think he was seeing the picturesque grass and trees.

Trin made the cocoa and got him a couple cookies. She set it all down in front of him, pulling a barstool up close. She touched his hand when he didn't move or reach for the food. "Your hands are freezing!" Taking one of his large hands between hers she rubbed them trying to warm them up.

Zander studied her in the dimly lit room. Suddenly, he stood, pulled her to her feet and tugged her against his chest. Trin was surprised, but she didn't resist. He was still trembling. She rubbed his bare back gently and rested her head in the crook of his neck. He clung to her, the strong muscles of his chest rubbing against her shoulder. For the first time, she ignored the romantic longings his touch stirred. He needed her and she could feel it.

Gradually, he seemed to calm down. When he finally pulled back, he muttered, "Thank you."

"Sure." It wasn't like the hug had been difficult for her, quite the opposite, but she didn't need to be thinking how attracted she was to him when he was obviously shaken.

He sat again and she gestured toward the food. He picked up the hot cocoa and sipped it. "Thank you, again."

"Are you okay? Can you tell me about it?"

Zander studied his mug. "I don't know if you want to hear it."

"Hey." She nudged his knee. "We're friends, remember? Friends help each other when they wake up in the night screaming." Kissing friends, if earlier today was any indication. They'd had a powerful connection. He wasn't going to shut her out now, was he?

He gave her half a smile then shook his head. "How much do you know about me?"

"What do you mean?" She felt like she knew far too much yet not enough.

"You said you watched *The Bachelor* and you know my dad pretty well. Have you Googled me?"

"Not on a weekly basis."

He did smile at that.

A few seconds ticked by then she asked, "Why?"

"Have you read the stories about my mom?"

Trin inhaled sharply. "A few. She was killed in The Hotel at Auburn University."

He nodded. "Did you know I found her?"

"I'm so sorry." Oh, my. She knew his mom was murdered and didn't even want to picture a young Zander finding her bloody and unresponsive. No wonder he'd turned to alcohol.

"It gets worse. It was my fault."

"What do you mean it was your fault? They found the murderer and convicted him." From what she'd read it was pre-meditated. The guy stole all her valuables, tortured, and killed her. It was horrific.

"Yeah, but ... I should've been with her, protected her." He studied his mug, not drinking it or touching the cookies. "My mom was, almost childlike. I mean, that sounds like she wasn't smart. She was, and she was great to be around, but Dad spoiled her. He took care of every little thing and he was a gentleman to the T. He always opened her door, paid for everything, escorted her everywhere like she was some fragile princess."

Trin smiled at the image. She wondered what her dad had been like. Her stepdad used to treat her mom like that, but he'd turned to other interests and definitely didn't exude gentlemanly behavior.

"I was recruited to some of the top schools in the nation to play football."

"I didn't know that." The abrupt conversation change didn't make sense, but Zander definitely wasn't himself tonight. "Did you play college then?"

He shook his head. "My parents came with me on recruiting trips all over the nation the fall of my senior year. When we got the invite to Auburn it was the same weekend as a real estate conference where my dad was the keynote speaker. I really wanted to go to Auburn, so my mom agreed to fly down here with me. She'd never been on a trip without my dad. He had to talk her through how to pick up a rental car." He smiled sadly.

"When my dad asked me to come back here a few weeks ago I couldn't believe it. I haven't been back since that happened. I just couldn't do it." He exhaled then continued his story, "I was too young to drive the rental car and Mom was scary behind the wheel. Luckily the Montgomery Airport was small and the university had everything set up for us. I loved the campus, the coaches, the other players. One night they were having a bonfire. My mom said she was fine to go back to the hotel by herself. I … I let her go because I was so selfish I wanted to go to that bonfire. Then when the guys asked me to go have a beer, I did that too. I didn't get back to the hotel until pretty late." He hung his head.

"She hadn't used the deadbolt or the chain because she was waiting for me to come back." He stopped and finally muttered, "I guess the guy recognized who she was and followed her. When he knocked on the door she opened it, maybe she thought he was an employee or me." His voice cracked and he cleared it. "He took her money and jewelry and ..." The silence stretched on then he finally muttered, "You can imagine the rest."

"I'm so sorry," she repeated. Trin's voice felt tight with emotion. To find someone you loved murdered.

"That's what the nightmare is." His voice was hollow. "Me finding her."

"Oh, Zander." Trin didn't know if it was her place, but she put her arms around his broad shoulders.

He laid his head against her shoulder and she held him like a very large child. Things were clicking into place quicker than she could do one of Turk's twenty-piece puzzles. The alcohol. The despair in his face. The inability to cope with real life. This man was very damaged and she was falling hard for him. She wanted to help him, but therapy for someone who'd been through this kind of trauma was miles above her pay grade. Selfishly, she wondered if a relationship with Zander was even possible.

CHAPTER 9

Trin didn't see Zander the next morning. He'd been planning a hundred-mile bike ride so she didn't expect him until later that afternoon. She was kind of nervous about how things would go between them now. Would his revelations of last night bring them closer or make things awkward between them? He'd walked her back to her room and hadn't said much as he gave her a brief hug goodnight.

"What are you daydreaming about now, girl? That hunky man?" Moriah pushed the housekeeping cart into the closet and came out into the kitchen where Trin was making herself a turkey sandwich.

"Maybe," Trin admitted.

"Well, daydream away. Don't let me stop you." Moriah whistled. "If a man like that came knocking on my door I'd be all, yes, please and can I have another?" Moriah swayed her hips and Trin couldn't help but laugh.

"Do you go out dancing every weekend?" Trin asked.

"I wish. Turk's not much for the dancing scene."

"You have moves that put the rest of us to shame."

"Thanks." Moriah beamed. "I was on the dance team in high

school. They had me do the solos. Always wished I could've had training, but no money for that. Had to pay Harrison's football fees."

"How's he doing?"

"You haven't heard? He is rocking Auburn U." She raised her hands
like a ref signaling a touchdown. "I'm so proud. We're going to a game
this weekend. They give him four free tickets to every home game.
You wanna come?"

"I wish. Who would watch this place?" She took a large bite of her
sandwich. Moriah's homemade bread and fresh veggies from her
garden made it heavenly.

Moriah gave her a strange look. "Mr. Zander told me you were
going to hire us some more help so you could take a break sometime."

"Oh, did he? I'm thinking about it."

"Well, don't think too hard. You're going to waste away in this old
house."

"No more than you." She slowly chewed another bite. She
supposed it was sad that she didn't get away more, but she was needed
here. A football game would be a lot of fun. If only Zander could go
with them, but that thought was shot down quickly. Football at
Auburn University would dredge up all kinds of awful memories.

"Yeah, well, I ain't got a choice," Moriah said. "Need the moolah so
my boy can be having a fun Christmas. Hey. Speaking of money. Mr.
Zander said he's going to start my overtime early if I work a little later
today and watch the front desk for you. You two got hot plans?"

"Not that I know of." Her stomach filled with excitement and a
little apprehension. Had Zander made plans for them? She didn't like
leaving her house for very long. "How late are you staying?"

"He said until after dinner. I'm going to go pick up Turk and bring
him here. That was part of the deal too. I could bring Turk to work."

"If you're bringing Turk here, I'm not leaving." Maybe that could
be her excuse to hang around. Why couldn't Zander just pickup
takeout and they could stay at the house together? They could make it
a party with Moriah and Turk.

"Hey, I know my kiddo is stinking cute, but if a handsome, rich man makes arrangements to get you away from work, you bet your skinny buns you're leaving."

She was right, but there was still a knot in Trin's stomach at the thought of not being here. "Go get Turk now so I can see him."

"Okay." Moriah grabbed her keys and slid out the back door.

Trin finished her sandwich and straightened up the kitchen. She wandered into her office and responded to emails and confirmed some reservation requests. Movement at the door pulled her eyes off her computer. Zander stood there, freshly showered but wearing a T-shirt and silky Under Armour shorts like he was planning on working out more. He looked … unreal handsome.

She stood and crossed the room to him. His eyes didn't betray any of the sorrow of last night. She didn't want to bring it up again, but wondered if he'd recovered from the nightmare and all the pain it had brought back.

"Hey," he said, reaching out for her hand.

Trin gladly gave it to him. He squeezed it softly and smiled. "Moriah's going to watch the place so you can have a break."

"She told me. What if I don't want a break?" She was partially teasing him.

He stared at her. "Please take a break with me, Trin?"

Trin's breath caught. The house would be okay with Moriah here. Maybe it was time she did escape with a handsome man like Moriah suggested. Yet, she couldn't help but tease him, "Oh, sorry. If I'm taking a break I need to go shopping for some new shoes and meet up with a guy I met online for drinks."

His face slackened and he blinked at her. "Are you … serious?"

Trin held it for a few seconds then burst out laughing. "No! Like I'd meet some guy for drinks. Of course I want to go with you."

He half-laughed then pulled her close and held her. Trin inhaled his delicious scent and didn't care if they went on a date, or just stayed right here and hugged. Actually, she'd prefer the latter.

He grasped her shoulders and held her back so he could look into her eyes. "Don't tease me like that. I about had heart failure thinking of you dating some dude you met online."

"I forget you had no siblings to learn how to take a tease."

"A quality I need to acquire for sure. How many siblings do you have?"

"I'm the oldest of four. So I basically initiated the teasing." She wasn't very close to her half-siblings now, but they'd had fun together when they were growing up.

"You're good at it. Go change quick."

"Into what?"

"Something comfortable."

"Okay." She grinned as she pulled away from him and slipped out the office door then outside. Changing quickly into a fitted T-shirt and yoga pants, she charged back out her apartment door and ran right into Marcus. He steadied her, his hands lingering on her arms.

"Hey, my beautiful boss. You in a hurry?"

"Yeah." She pulled back, wondering if she needed to correct his unprofessional comment. "Everything going okay?"

"Sure. I'm almost through the list from yesterday. You'd think eventually nothing else could break, but I guess not."

"I'm just grateful you're so handy."

Marcus took a step closer and his green eyes twinkled at her. "I'm good at a lot of things."

"I'm sure you are. I need to go."

"Oh ... Okay." His voice said he didn't think it was okay.

She scurried around him, but could feel his eyes on her back. Marcus had hinted a few times that he was interested, but Trin definitely wasn't. He was a nice-looking, fit guy, but she was busy with her work. Zander was leaning against the back door. Okay, so maybe she was making an exception for another nice-looking, fit guy.

Zander's eyes flitted over her head. She turned to see Marcus still watching her. He and Zander locked gazes and Trin could almost feel the battle of wills. Marcus turned away and stomped to the shed.

"Was he bothering you?" Zander asked.

She shook her head. The last thing she needed was some silly guy struggle over her, or Marcus getting fired because Zander thought he was hitting on her. Marcus would be back on the streets without this job and this place to stay. She wasn't going to do that to him, and she could handle a few innuendos.

Zander's lips pursed, but he didn't say anything more about it. He took her hand and they walked side by side to his Audi. "Is this your car?" she asked, never having thought about it before.

"Just a rental." He smiled. "Funny, but I don't own a car."

"Seriously?"

"I'm a wanderer. I have a condo in Midtown, New York, but I'm rarely there and when I go there it's just easier to walk or call an Uber."

"Yeah, but you probably use the Uber Black or whatever the most expensive one is."

He shrugged and opened her door. Trin settled into the car, once again feeling the gap between them. Mr. Keller paid her well, but she wasn't using Uber Black to get around. Thinking about Mr. Keller made her wonder if Zander had called him yet. He'd promised last night over dinner that he would.

He climbed in and gave her a smile. They were both quiet on the drive until they pulled into Vaughan Road Park. Trin turned to him. "I used to come here with my grandparents."

"So, is this a good memory place or do you want to go somewhere else?"

"It's a great memory. I told you how much I love my grandparents." This made her feel almost as comfortable as her house. It was that connection that kept her going.

He parked the car and focused on her. "Yeah. I, just, I don't like to go anywhere I used to go with my mom."

"Oh." She sat back against the seat. "I see." She didn't know what to say. Maybe it was because her grandparents had lived full lives when they died and they weren't murdered and she didn't find them dead. She shook her head and wished she had some way to help him.

He swung open the door. She placed a hand on his arm and he turned to her. "Zander? Have you ever thought of getting some professional help?"

"My dad set me up with a counselor after my mom died."

"Did it help?"

"I don't know. I never went to the appointments."

So that was no help. "Did your … recovery center have someone professional you could talk to about … things?"

Zander nodded. "Don't worry, Trin. I'm doing okay." He climbed out of the car and walked around to open her door.

Trin didn't know how to tell him that she wanted to help him be better than okay. She was just okay too, working her life away and never realizing what she was missing until Zander came along. Could they find something more … together? She was getting way ahead of the relationship.

She stepped out of the car and he shut her door then popped his trunk and pulled out tennis rackets and balls. Trin's stomach did a happy leap. "Oh, Zander. I love tennis. How did you know? Moriah again?"

"No. You told me you played for Huntingdon College, remember?"

"Oh, yeah."

They walked to the tennis courts and he handed her a racket. Trin hadn't played much since she'd graduated a couple of years ago and suddenly worried that she was going to be horrible. They hit around for a few minutes to warmup and then started a game. Trin fell back into her serve and swing quickly. She beat Zander soundly the first couple of games, but then he warmed up and gave her a solid run for the next two games.

"Have you played much?" she asked him as they stopped for a drink of water. She was sweaty and tired and it felt glorious. This was the type of fun she hadn't allowed herself since she graduated and started managing the bed and breakfast.

"My mom taught me when I was pretty young, but it's been a lot of years since I picked up a racket."

"You're really good," she said.

"Let's get married."

"Wh-what?" Trin's heart and voice both stuttered.

"We'd have really athletic children." Zander grinned, his eyes twinkling like he knew what she'd been thinking, or fantasizing.

"If that's all that's important to you," she said stiffly.

"Of course it is. Every guy wants athletic children."

She shook her head and couldn't help but laugh. "Did you play college football?"

"No." His eyes got a faraway look. "I couldn't after ... everything that happened. NYU never gave me an offer anyway." He shrugged.

"So you lived at home? Or was that too far of a commute?"

Zander eyed her strangely. "I thought I'd told you."

"Told me what?"

"I haven't been in my parents' home since my mother's funeral."

Trin studied him and swallowed hard. This man most definitely needed someone to help him deal with his trauma, but she wasn't about to suggest that to him for the second time in a day.

"Let's play."

She picked up her racket and jogged to the court. All of her thoughts earlier about making something work together were definitely wishful thinking. Zander was a great guy and she enjoyed being around him, but a serious relationship with someone with his traumatic emotional history was probably never going to happen. That thought shouldn't be as devastating as thinking about her house being sold.

CHAPTER 10

Zander snuck into the kitchen late in the morning of November twentieth. In a week he was going to have to fly to Australia to get acclimatized and settled for his race, but he was taking advantage of every moment with Trin before that. After he completed his training each day he helped her with whatever work she had to do then they played tennis when Moriah could be there in the early afternoon. Trin seemed to be getting more comfortable leaving the house so that made him happy.

Unfortunately, his dad was still being deliberately vague and wouldn't give Zander a straight answer when he called and asked if he was selling the house or replacing Trin. Why didn't his dad want to help him make Trin feel confident in her job? It was making Zander crazy, but probably making Trin even more crazy. The Cloverdale was so much more than a job to her and he suspected she worked so hard to prove her worth.

Despite that worry in the back of both of their minds, almost every night he'd pick up takeout or they'd cook dinner together. It was a comfortable pattern that he didn't want to end, but she'd balked the one time he asked her to leave the house for longer than an hour or two to play tennis. He hoped she'd go with him tonight, and since she hadn't hired an evening and night manager yet like he'd asked her to, he had to enlist Moriah's help. It frustrated him she wouldn't even try to hire somebody, he was about ready to go over her head and do it, but she claimed she'd had some shoddy help in the past and had to be careful. It was really that she didn't trust anybody else with her house. It was a miracle she'd brought Marcus on like she had.

Moriah was singing as she mixed up dough of some sort in a large bowl.

"Hey," Zander said.

She jumped and whirled, laughing. "Boy! You sneaky thing. What's going on? Where's my girl? You two are never apart lately."

That was exactly how Zander liked it. He needed Trin close by more than he'd ever needed a glass of vodka. "In her office doing paperwork."

"You fancying something sweet to eat?"

"No." He held up his hands. "If I keep eating all your treats I'm not even going to be able to complete my Ironman let alone place." The triathlons he'd participated in the last two weekends hadn't been PRs and he could definitely blame the sugar. He'd relaxed too much with his diet over the past few weeks.

She laughed. "Who cares? Sugar's better than a medal any day."

Zander couldn't help but smile at the feisty, cute girl. He'd gained two friends at this welcoming house and he was loathe to leave next week. "I need a favor."

"Tell me and I'll fulfill it."

"I want to take Trin on a real date. I keep bugging her to hire more help but she hasn't done it yet and I'm tired of waiting."

"What you got in mind?" She was still smiling, but her voice was a little wary.

"I know there's a vacancy in one of the rooms tonight. Could you bring Turk here to stay? I'll buy you pizza, pay you extra, and get you passes for the Montgomery Zoo."

Moriah's smile widened. "I would've done it for the pizza, but good heavens, I ain't gonna turn the rest down. Sure thing. Let me finish these cookies and go pick up my little man."

"You're a saint. Let me know when you're back and I'll kidnap her."

"Now that's a plan I can get down with."

Zander thanked her and edged out of the kitchen. He glimpsed Trin in her office. She already looked gorgeous with her dark red hair hanging in waves down her back and a silky button down blue shirt over some patterned leggings. She walked out of the office and toward him and he found himself once again admiring her legs.

"I bribed Moriah for some time alone with you."

"Oh?" She smiled and her beautiful face lit up. "Are we playing tennis or something? I can go change."

"No. She's going to bring Turk here for an overnight party and you and I are going on a date."

"An overnight date?" Concern filled her voice.

"No. Just a regular go out to dinner, kiss in the moonlight type of date." Overnight? No way. The few times he'd kissed Trin had been an explosion of emotion, passion, and sensation. He was amazed either of them had been able to stop at kissing. He'd had a lot of different women come onto him over the years, especially when he was on *The Bachelor*, but he hadn't let anyone get close. Now that he was becoming such good friends with Trin and wanting so much more, he had to be careful or he'd become more addicted to her than any substance and never recover if things went wrong. He was a wanderer and Trin was married to this house. He couldn't get enough of her, but reality had to come into play at some point.

She relaxed and squeezed his hand. "Sounds great. Let me finish up these reservation requests and some billing issues then I'll freshen up and we can go."

"Perfect. We have to wait for Moriah to come back with Turk anyway."

TRIN WAS TRYING to relax and enjoy this time with Zander, but she truly hated being away from her house. Like it was her firstborn son or something. She almost felt like she needed to prove to Zander, and maybe to herself, that she could take a break. She knew he was frustrated that she hadn't hired any more help, but it was hard to trust just anyone with her house.

Zander took her to dinner at Jalapeños. Trin had the carne asada. The beef was tender and succulent, but it was the creamy guacamole that she couldn't get enough of. She and Zander talked easily during dinner and then sauntered down the nearby Riverwalk. She could do this, she could be away and be okay. She just hoped Moriah was doing all right.

The river was so peaceful tonight. There were some families and couples walking around. Zander held her close to his side and whispered, "I wanted to have a romantic spot to kiss you, but I don't want a ten-year old as my audience." He gestured to a blond boy walking past who stuck out his tongue at them.

Trin laughed. "Anywhere with you is romantic."

"Yeah?" Zander arched an eyebrow. "Let's get back home quick then." He steered her toward the stairs.

Home. She wanted to kiss him right there for the mere suggestion. Was Zander coming to feel about her house the way she did? It was home and it was love and happiness. Maybe there was hope for them if he cared about her house as much as she did, and would help her keep it even if his dad had different plans.

Zander held her hand, but didn't say much on the drive home. The tension in the air was palpable. It seemed he wanted to kiss her as badly as she wanted to be kissed.

He pulled into the guest parking, jammed the car into park, and jumped out of his door. Seconds later, he was opening her door and offering his hand. Trin shivered from anticipation and she couldn't help but admit to herself that she was glad to be home. She placed her hand in his and he tugged her out of the car, shut the door behind her and then pinned her against the car with a hand on each side of her head and his body flush against hers.

"My, my, Mr. Keller," she whispered. "You act like a man who hasn't tasted a pair of lips in a while."

"You have no idea how thirsty I am for you, Ms. Dean."

She giggled. He smiled and trailed a hand along her cheek and into her hair. Trin leaned into his touch. Zander bent down and gently tasted her lips. Trin clasped her hands around his neck and pulled him in tighter. Zander groaned and deepened the kiss. Exhilaration shot through her. They were reaching new levels of intimacy and she was not going to complain for a second. The kiss continued until she was breathless and could hardly stand on her own two feet.

Zander pulled away and studied her. "Thank you for going to dinner with me," he said formally, offering her his elbow.

They walked toward the back yard and her apartment. The moonlight caressed the strong planes of his handsome face. "It was my pleasure, Mr. Keller."

They reached her door and he turned toward her. "Trin, I absolutely loved that kiss, but you calling me Mr. Keller has me thinking of my dad and … not a great thing right now."

She laughed, but then she thought of his dad too. "Isn't it weird to you that he won't tell you why he sent you here?"

"Trin, don't worry so much."

That was easy for him to say, this house wasn't his livelihood and connection to family.

"Maybe he just wanted me to have a relaxing place to train," Zander said.

"If that's true, why would he tell you to do an *Undercover Boss* situation?"

"I don't know." He jammed his hand through his short, dark hair. "But you're worrying too much."

"If someone might rip your life out from under you, you'd worry too."

He reached for her shoulders and gently caressed down her arms. "You don't know my dad like I do. When he's ready, he'll tell me what he's thinking, but I promise you that I'm going to make it good for you. He'll do whatever I ask."

She pulled back, the thought of her house being sold or her being fired ticking her off. "Oh, yeah, I forgot. Your father has never told you no, why would he start now?" Oh, my, that was low and she sounded bitter, but honestly silver spoons were nothing compared to how Zander had been raised.

His mouth pursed. "I'm trying to help you."

"I appreciate that, but maybe at some point you should think about helping yourself."

"What does that mean?"

"Get some help, Zander." She was mad, but she was also concerned about him. "You know your mom wouldn't want you to blame yourself and not think you can move on. You could do so much good with your money, your looks, your influence, but you hide yourself away, don't make any lasting friendships or give yourself completely. Are you going to be able to stay committed to us or am I a fling like alcohol or your training?"

Zander backed away. Trin wanted to take the words back. But maybe he needed to hear them, and okay, she was a little torqued at him right now. Her entire existence was being threatened and he told her to relax? How would he feel if someone uprooted his hopes and dreams? Wait. He didn't seem to have any roots. He hadn't gone home in ten years.

He said nothing, simply stared at her for a few uncomfortable seconds then walked toward the Cloverdale.

Trin's anger burst into a heat that had her walking around the back yard to try and cool down. How dare he tell her not to worry? The day she'd turned eighteen her stepdad had given her a hundred dollar bill and told her she was on her own. She would've left home anyway, but being kicked out like that and knowing she had to survive on her own was terrifying. She'd spent every minute trying to prove that she was worth something. Zander had no clue what it was like, scraping an existence out of nothing, losing the Cloverdale when her mom sold it, the only home she'd ever cared about, then having his dad give her the opportunity to manage it and stay in the one spot where she'd felt unconditional love.

Yet she should go apologize to him. He obviously had post-traumatic stress disorder from seeing his mom murdered and never dealing with it. If she was truly falling for him like she thought she was, she needed to be more understanding with him and what he could deal with. He'd been through more horrible trauma at seventeen than she could even imagine. He was doing good things with his life, just because she was slightly jealous of the increased good he could do, didn't mean he had to do it. Maybe. Yet she still wanted him to get past the pain so they could have hope at a healthy relationship. Oh, she was so confused.

She was on her fifth round of the yard when a shadow suddenly darted out from behind a huge oak tree and grabbed her arm. She screamed out. He tugged her back under the tree.

"Zander!" Trin hit his arm, but he didn't let her go. Why would he pull a juvenile trick like scaring her when he knew she was mad at him? "Don't scare me like that."

He pushed her against the bark of the tree and Trin gasped. It wasn't Zander. It was Marcus, but it was a Marcus she hadn't met often. His eyes were glassed over and he was weaving on his feet. "So pretty," he murmured, pushing his body up against hers, his arms clamping securely around her back.

"Marcus," Trin said sternly, squirming away from his touch, but having nowhere to go with his body pressing her into the tree. "Let me go," she said it slowly and clearly, hoping he was with it enough to understand the command.

"No, ma'am." His hot breath was on her neck then he licked her.

Trin gagged. Disgusting.

"Let me go or I will fire you."

"Don't care about the job. Been wanting you for a long, long time," he slurred out.

Cold terror raced down Trin's spine. He was lucid enough, but either the alcohol had a hold of him or he had been planning this and needed the boost of being drunk to give him courage.

She screamed at the top of her lungs, praying someone would hear her.

With surprising strength and quickness Marcus kicked her legs out from under her and slammed her back into the ground. She gasped in pain and shock as Marcus dropped on top of her. His mouth came down hard on hers, muffling her screams. Trin could hardly breathe with the pressure of his larger frame on top of her. One of her arms was pinned between them, but she kicked, and hit at him with her free arm. He didn't seem to notice. His breath was foul and tasted of strong alcohol. Trin bit his lip hard between her teeth.

He howled, pulled his head back and slammed his forehead into hers. Pain burst through her head and the world went black for a few horrible seconds. Marcus grabbed her face between his hands and slammed her head into the unforgiving ground. Trin cried out. She was going to pass out and if she did, he could ravage her body without any struggle from her. She whispered a short prayer for help, but didn't hold out much hope as she tried to buck her hips and flail against him. He was too heavy, too strong.

He had her head in his hands again and she didn't know that she'd stay conscious through another hit to her head.

"Hey!" she heard a voice through the fog, an angry, male voice. Zander? She could only pray it was him. She was so out of it, she might be imagining things.

Marcus pivoted while still on top of her and the pressure of his body ground her into the grass. Trin groaned. Marcus was lifted off of her and she heard as much as saw his body flung against the tree trunk. He slumped down. The man lifted him up to his feet and drove his fist into his face. Marcus looked like a limp doll. The man let go of him and he slid to the ground.

The man turned to her as Trin struggled to sit up. Zander. She muttered a prayer of thanks.

"Trin, no, what did he do to you?" Zander's arms were around her and he gently lifted her off the ground, carrying her back to the main house like she weighed nothing more than a child.

"I'm okay," Trin muttered. "He didn't, you know." She laid her head against Zander's chest, his warm scent and strong body comforting her as if she'd come home at Christmastime. Christmas was a little over a month away. Would Zander even be here then? She closed her eyes, realizing her thoughts were erratic. She'd just been attacked by her employee and she was worried about if Zander would be hanging up Christmas stockings with her. Dumb.

Zander swung the front door open then carried her into the sitting room and set her on a couch.

"I heard some screaming," Mr. Gunnell said from behind Zander. "Everything okay?"

"Marcus attacked Trin. Can you call 911? I left him in the backyard unconscious."

Mr. Gunnell's eyes widened. "No! I'll call right now." He pulled out his cell phone and walked away, giving them a little privacy.

Zander knelt down and brushed the hair from her face. "Are you okay, love? Do you need an ambulance?"

Love? Had Zander just called her love? "No," she lied. "I just want to lay here."

"I'll be right back." Zander stood and rushed to the kitchen.

She wanted to lie here, but she wanted him to stay close. Had she told him that or not? Everything was pretty fuzzy right now.

Zander returned with a wet towel and a glass of water. "Here, love." He held her up and pressed the cup to her lips. "Drink this."

She sipped a little bit. The cool water slid down her throat, recharging her. "Thank you."

He helped her lay back down and put the cold towel on her forehead. It felt almost as wonderful as his hands touching her.

"The police are on their way," Mr. Gunnell said from somewhere in the room. Everything was distorted. "I'm going outside to make sure that weasel doesn't escape if he wakes up."

Zander stood. "Are you sure? I can go." He glanced back down at Trin and she held up her hand to him.

"I've got this." Mr. Gunnell stood straight. "Take care of our girl."

Trin wondered what Mr. Gunnell would do if Marcus woke up with any fight left in him. The old man would be no match for him. But selfishly she wanted Zander here with her.

Zander knelt down next to the couch again. He cupped her cheek with his hand and stared at her. Trin blinked up at him. The world was clearing and his perfectly handsome face was the one thing she wanted to look at.

"Thank you for coming," she whispered.

"I heard you scream."

"I'm glad I can scream loud." She tried to smile but it fell flat.

Zander glanced over her face and shuddered. "The police will bring EMTs and they can check you out, make sure you're okay."

"I'm okay. He head-butted me then slammed my head into the ground, but everything's clear now."

"You might have a concussion."

"Probably just a huge headache."

She closed her eyes for a second and savored his fingers caressing her cheek, his wonderful scent surrounding her. "Just stay with me, please."

"Of course."

Sirens wailed in the distance. The police would come and take Marcus and she wouldn't have to worry about him hurting her anymore. For some reason tears leaked out of the corners of her eyes. Marcus—dumb kid throwing his life away. Even though he'd attacked her, she had a hard time not feeling sorry for him. He'd had a hard life and he'd been under the influence.

"Does it hurt?" The words ripped out of Zander. "I can't stand for you to hurt."

Trin opened her eyes to see Zander studying her with far too much concern. "No. I just feel bad for Marcus."

"For Marcus? I told you to fire him. You have no idea how unpredictable somebody under the influence can be."

"I was trying to help him. He's had a hard life."

"I'll give him a hard life," Zander muttered. "You weren't helping him. You were putting yourself at risk. Nobody can help somebody like that except for a treatment center. But he deserves prison after what he did to you."

"He's just a dumb kid who has nobody to look out for him," she said from between clenched teeth. "I would think you of all people would understand being intoxicated and making poor choices."

His hands fell from her face. He reared back onto his heels. "I never hurt someone while under the influence," he muttered.

The sirens descended on the house and Zander stood to go meet the police. Chaos ensued as guests came out of their beds to see what had happened and the police and EMTs were all over Trin. Luckily, they said she might have a mild concussion but didn't force her to go to the hospital. Zander promised he'd watch over her. True to his word, he stayed close by, but there were no more references of love and there was a hardness in his eyes she knew she'd put there.

CHAPTER 11

Zander carried all his luggage down the stairs the next morning. He hated to leave Trin after her being hurt and now she would have even less help with the bed and breakfast with Marcus in jail. Yet at the same time he needed to go now. Seeing her attacked had brought back too many feelings and memories of his mom. Plus, Trin didn't respect him or understand that he was dealing with what he'd gone through the only way he could ... Not thinking about it.

He loved the time he'd spent here, but his race in Australia was the perfect reason to escape before he or Trin said more things they'd regret. She was right in thinking they were from different worlds. Whether those worlds could ever intersect was anyone's guess. He didn't know, but he did know walking out this door was going to be as hard as admitting himself to Tranquility Woods. He'd become more addicted to Trin than he had to any substance. She was the best high he'd ever had and it was natural, like his training. Now he was walking away to protect his heart from shattering when they couldn't reconcile their differences. Maybe someday he'd come back. Maybe not.

She wasn't in her office. He slipped out the front door and loaded up his rental then turned back to the house, steeling himself to say goodbye.

Trin stood on the porch, watching him. "Were you going to leave without saying goodbye?"

He slowly walked back, stopping at the bottom of the stairs. "I wouldn't do that."

She moved to the edge of the steps, but didn't descend them.

"How are you feeling?" he asked. She had some bruising above her eyes, but she looked pretty good, considering what she'd been through.

"Nothing a little ibuprofen won't fix." She wrapped one hand around the porch railing. "So ... Australia?"

"Yeah."

"And then where?"

Zander studied her, wishing he knew that she wanted him to fly back to her as quickly as possible. "I don't know."

She nodded. "Thank you for being here."

"Thank you for having me." Zander didn't know if this goodbye could get any worse.

"Well then." She was still hanging on to the railing like it was her lifeline.

Zander had never felt so awkward. Was he supposed to turn and go? Or was there any possibility he could rush up those porch steps, sweep her into his arms, and give her a goodbye kiss she'd never forget?

Her eyes were filled with as much uncertainty as he felt. He slowly pushed out a breath and raised a hand. This was hard, but he was strong. "Goodbye, Trin."

She gave a little gasp and ran down the stairs, throwing herself into his arms, and about knocking him off his feet. Zander recovered from the shock quickly, holding her close and capturing her mouth with his own. The explosion of light and joy raced through him that he'd started to expect when he held her and kissed her. He wanted her, all of her. He couldn't possibly let her go.

She pulled back and he forced himself to release her though it was harder than dumping his last bottle of Jack Daniels down the kitchen sink. "Goodbye," she whispered then ran back up the stairs and slammed the front door.

Zander didn't know how long he stood there staring at the door. The etched glass and wood that had been so welcoming, but now was closed to him, shutting him out.

Part of him wanted to forget about the race he'd been training for the past few months, bang through that door, and sweep her off her feet, but the rational part knew they had a lot of barriers separating them. Her unwillingness to understand his lifestyle and his unwillingness to change his lifestyle. Not to mention her unsympathetic insistence he get help to overcome his mother's death and her unbreakable bonds to this house. Neither one of them were good at relationships or had much hope of making one last.

He finally turned and plodded to his car. He would be in airplanes and airports for the next day and a half, but that misery didn't even come closing to wondering if he'd ever have Trin in his arms again.

CHAPTER 12

The next week and a half was horrible for Trin, but she got a lot accomplished. Zander was gone and the hole in her happiness was huge. She'd gotten so used to him being with her throughout the day, and though she teased him about not knowing how to work, he really did know how, and he'd lightened her load considerably. Thanksgiving was a lonely affair and she had a hard time being thankful for much of anything.

She'd gotten a text from him Saturday, December third.

Australia is beautiful. Miss you. Please call my dad and hire some help.

He missed her. Ahh. Yet why did he have to tell her what to do? She didn't tell him, go get a therapist so you can learn how to form lasting relationships. Well, she had said something close to that, but she wasn't texting it.

Miss you too. Good luck in the race.

Thanks.

Monday morning, she and Moriah had finished breakfast and cleanup and Moriah was straightening rooms by herself while Trin tried to take care of the yard. She'd made a list of all the projects that needed to be done this morning and knew she'd have to call a repairman. It was little things like one of the outlets in the dining room needed to be replaced and the vacuum wasn't sucking properly. She didn't miss Marcus after what he'd done, but she sure missed his handy skills.

She hadn't called Zander's dad, half-terrified of what he had to say to her so she kept putting it off. She was dying to know how Zander's race had gone and if he would come back here, but she didn't want to be the one to instigate anything. She'd flung herself at him before he left, and though the kiss was amazing, she really had no clue how to accept him for who he was. She loved him, but was that enough to make it work? Did he even care to make it work anymore?

Her phone beeped. She rested against her rake and pulled it out of her pocket. Her heart leapt when she saw it was him.

Race was miserable. Miss you. Why haven't you called my dad yet?

She smiled yet prickled at the same time. He didn't need to push her.

Sorry about the race. I'm sure you did better than you think.

Not really. Too many of Moriah's cookies. Tell her I blame her.

She fully smiled then.

I will.

His only response was a smiley face.

She kept her phone out and pulled up Peter Keller in the contacts. Maybe she just needed to do it before she lost her nerve. Zander either didn't know why Mr. Keller sent him to her or didn't want to tell her. Was this her moment of truth? She would rather keep dealing with things than have a heart-to-heart with her boss. She just couldn't lose her house.

She swallowed and noticed her hand was trembling over the screen. Before she could second-guess the decision she pushed the call button. The phone started ringing and she almost cancelled the call, but Mr. Keller's cultured voice came through before she could, "Trin! How are you?"

"I'm good, thank you, sir."

"Zander had great things to say about you."

"H-he did?"

"Yes, he did, but he tells me you're working yourself too hard."

Trin shook her head then remembered he couldn't see her. "I love this place, you know that, sir."

"Yes, I do, which is why I've decided to give you part-ownership."

Trin's legs buckled and she slowly sank onto the dead grass. Had she really heard what she thought she'd heard? "Excuse me?"

Mr. Keller chuckled and it sounded so much like Zander she found herself clutching the phone tighter. "Zander made the suggestion and I really liked it. Actually, if it was up to him he'd give you the house outright."

Oh, Zander. If he cared that much about her, why didn't he tell her he was coming back now that his race was over?

"I'm going to send you some paperwork after the lawyers finish with it. Look it over and if it meets your specifications, sign it and send it back."

"Okay," she managed.

"Basically I'm making you part-owner, giving you profit-sharing and bonuses based on profitability."

"Wow. Okay." She knew the bed and breakfast was profitable. There was no debt on the property and the rooms rented for a substantial amount each night.

"But, you need to get some help hired, today. I want the maintenance man and gardener replaced, but I especially want one or two housekeepers on staff as well as someone to man the desk so you can take a break. Oh, and give Moriah a raise and I want her to focus on baking, cooking, and learning management skills from you so we can move her into a management position at Cloverdale or one of my other properties. Make sure she doesn't need to work overtime and let's figure out some bonuses she can earn. From what Zander says she deserves it. I'll increase your employee budget, but leave the details up to you."

Zander. He must've had quite the talk with his dad about the Cloverdale.

"Thanks for your dedication. I trust you, Trin and you've done a wonderful job."

"Thank you, Mr. Keller."

"We'll be in touch soon."

The phone call disconnected but Trin didn't move from the grass. Mr. Keller had just given her part ownership of her grandparent's house. He trusted her. She glanced at her house. Her house. It really was now. Zander wanted her to have the entire house. Oh, she liked him.

Moriah leaned out the kitchen door. "What are you doing laying in the grass?"

Trin jumped to her feet and ran to her friend, hugging her then pulling back and grabbing her hands. "Mr. Keller made me part-owner and he's giving you a raise and bonuses! You're going to bake, cook, and learn about management."

Moriah jumped up in the air. "Yeah, baby!"

"You have to only work full-time though."

"Oh, thank the good Lord. I want to be home with my boy more."

"Plus, we're hiring a lot more help. That'll be the tough part. I hate finding good help."

"Didn't Zander tell you to hire more help weeks ago?"

"Yeah." She sighed and smiled at her friend. "I think Zander is behind all of this."

"You gonna give him a kiss of gratitude or should I?" Moriah winked.

"We both can if he ever comes back."

"Oh, he'll come back. I saw the way he checked you out, girl, and you got nothin' to worry about."

Trin laughed and squeezed her friend's hands. "We'll see. I'm going to ignore the leaves and start calling around to some employment services. I wonder if the college might have some students looking for part-time."

"Good idea. Get to work finding us some help so I can get home to my boy."

"First, I need to send Zander a quick text thank you."

"Don't you think that should be a phone call?"

"Wish I was that brave, but no."

Moriah rolled her eyes and headed back inside. "Your loss. Hopefully he'll be here soon and you can give him lip to lip thanks."

Trin warmed at the thought of that. She pulled out her phone and texted,

Talked to your dad. Thank you! Wish I could thank you in person. I'm walking on clouds here.

His text back was almost immediate.

You deserve it. Congrats! I'll talk to you soon.

So what was soon in his mind? Trin knew keeping this place running with just her and Moriah as well as interviewing and training would keep her busy, but she'd rather see Zander than anything else on her to-do list.

CHAPTER 13

Zander's plane landed in Montgomery late Friday afternoon. He
should've been back a couple of days ago, but he'd let his body
recover before taking the long plane ride back. Even in first class
accommodations, there was nothing as miserable as traveling when
your body ached from a hard race. He grabbed his luggage and rental
car and drove straight to the bed and breakfast.

He'd kept the texts to Trin to a minimum, even though he missed
her horribly and wanted to be with her. Her impulsive kiss on the
front porch was one of the few indicators that she wanted him in her
life. He didn't have enough experience with real relationships to know
how to proceed in a way that wouldn't be too much too fast. He had to
go with instinct and his desire to be with her and hope she felt the
same and they could work out their differences.

Parking in a visitor space, he saw Trin's Accord parked to the side
of the house. She was here. He smiled to himself. Of course she was,
he'd never met someone who loved their work this much, besides his
dad, but he also assumed that was because work was the only thing
that helped his dad forget his mom.

He jumped from his rented sport utility and climbed the stairs
with a spring in his step. He'd be seeing Trin any minute. Pushing

through the front door, his smile faltered for a second when it was Moriah not Trin at the desk. Turk was pushing a truck around on the floor behind the desk. The little man had short black curls and a smile as large as his mom's.

"Hey, Moriah. What's up, Turk, my man?"

Turk's head came up and he dodged around the desk and gave Zander a pound. "Throw?" he asked.

Zander lifted him up and tossed him into the air, amidst peals of laughter. Zander joined in the laughter and threw him a few more times before holding him against his side.

"Thanks, Zander. He misses my big brother teasing with him."

"Anytime." Zander turned Turk upside down and held him by one leg.

Turk giggled. "Up, up!"

Zander complied, lifting him above his head and using him for some triceps extensions.

"Why are you working so late?" he asked Moriah, who was beaming at her child. "I thought Trin hired more help."

"She did and they're working out great, but everybody else needed the night off tonight, and if Turk can come with me, I don't mind doing a night once in a while."

"That's great of you. So Trin isn't working tonight?" He gave Turk one more toss and a brief squeeze then set him on the floor.

"Thanks you, sir," the toddler said.

Zander chuckled. "You teach them sir and ma'am young."

"Yes, sir." Moriah smiled.

"Where's Trin then?"

"Um, she's downtown. I think at the Riverwalk. There's some Christmas activities going on."

"Oh, good, she finally listened to me and is taking a break." He just wished she was taking it with him. He'd go find her. He couldn't wait any longer. "I'm glad the new staff is working out well."

"Couldn't be better, thank you and thank you for the raise."

"You deserved it. I'm going to go find her."

"Okay, um, maybe you should just wait and see her in the morning."

Moriah was definitely not acting like herself, but it'd been a couple weeks since he'd been here and maybe she was just surprised to see him show up without warning. "I can't wait." He smiled at her. "I didn't even ask. Do you have a room for me?"

"Yes. We had someone check out this morning."

"Great. Thank you." He handed over a credit card.

Moriah finally chuckled at him. "That's kind of counter-productive. Paying for a room at your own place."

"It's not my place. It's my father's and Trin's."

"She's very happy about it." She handed him his card back.

"I'll see you in a little bit." Zander waved to Turk and hurried back out the door. He drove downtown, parked at the garage next to the Riverwalk and hurried across the ramp and down the stairs. Couples were walking along the river, Christmas music was playing, and vendors were selling nuts, popcorn, hot cocoa, and coffee. The weather was still nice, definitely not like Christmastime at home in New York, but there was a festive feeling in the air and Christmas lights and decorations strung around.

He searched for Trin, but didn't see her until he'd passed the spot where the Harriett II Riverboat was docked, a different Christmas song streaming from her decks as people disembarked from their dinner cruise.

Leaning against the railing was the unmistakable deep red hair and long, lean body of the woman he'd been dreaming about for the past two weeks. She looked so good, he could hardly restrain himself from running to her. She stared into the water, not looking at anyone around her.

Zander approached her from the side and softly spoke her name, "Trin."

She whirled to him and her eyes widened. "Zander! You're back!"

He grinned and couldn't resist wrapping his hands around her waist and sweeping her off her feet. She put back her head and laughed and Zander wondered how he'd ever left her.

"You're back," she said again.

"I'm back." He lowered her body against his and stared at her beautiful face. "I missed you."

She smiled almost shyly. "I could tell by all the phone calls and texts."

"Sorry. I'm horrible with communication."

"Not every form of communication."

"Really? Which part am I good at?"

"Mouth to mouth."

Zander let out a surprised laugh, but took the hint very literally, leaning down and pressing his lips to hers. Trin sighed and her mouth parted. He wasted no time bringing her closer and increasing the pressure of the kiss.

"Trin?" A deep voice came from the side.

Trin jerked back and Zander was forced to release her mouth, but he kept one arm around her.

"Um, hey, Harrison," she said. "You're ... back."

The huge, good-looking black man held aloft two Styrofoam cups. "Should I have bought three?" His face was solemn as he regarded the two of them.

Zander looked from the guy who had just bought *his* girl a cup of cocoa back to his girl, awaiting some kind of explanation. He was gone a little over two weeks and she was dating someone else? Why the kiss, the excitement to see him? He stepped away from her and extended his hand. "Sorry. I'm Zander Keller. A friend of Trin's."

Harrison shifted both cups to his left hand. His palms were definitely large enough to hold more than two cups. He shook Zander's hand with a firm grip. "Nice to meet you. That's a very *friendly* greeting you two were having."

Zander looked to Trin, but she was staring at him like he should salvage the situation. He felt a bit of anger stir up in him. "We haven't seen each other in a long time."

The younger man smiled. "Glad to know you're so friendly, Trin."

Zander's anger flared. She'd better not even think about being *friendly* with anyone but him.

"Harrison plays football for Auburn."

Zander's eyebrows rose. "Really? Isn't that ironic."

She nodded. Harrison handed her the hot cocoa cup and she clamped her hands around it. "He's also Moriah's brother."

"Oh." Zander turned to Harrison. "Moriah's great. I know she's very proud of you."

"Yeah." The kid ducked his head. "She and my mom take proud to a new level."

He suddenly seemed very young to Zander, but he guessed Harrison was closer to Trin's age than he was. What a gut punch, to find her, kiss her, and then find she was on a date with someone else.

"They should be proud of you," Trin inserted.

Zander glanced back at her. Was she serious about this guy? He seemed like a great guy, but he was still in college. Didn't Trin want a man?

"Harrison's going to graduate in the spring as an accounting major. He's already got a job secured with Jackson Thornton."

"If I pass my CPA," Harrison inserted with a shy smile.

"You will. You're smarter than anybody I know."

Zander could not get a read on this situation. Was she dating Harrison or did she look at him like a little brother, okay a huge little brother, but still.

The silence kind of stretched and Zander knew he was worse than a third wheel. He was a third wheel who wanted to steal the guy's date.

"It was nice to meet you, Harrison." He turned to Trin. "Will I see you back at the bed and breakfast?"

"Sure, we'll talk in the morning. Harrison and I are going to *A Christmas Carol* tonight."

"Oh, okay. Well, you two *kids* have fun."

Trin's eyes flashed at him.

"Thank you." Harrison extended his hand again and Zander was forced to shake one more time. "It was nice to meet you, sir."

Sir. Zander suddenly felt like he was twenty years older than this kid and definitely not in the running for Trin's attention.

"Goodbye, Zander," Trin said.

Zander couldn't find it in him to say goodbye. He nodded to them, turned, and strode away. That had not gone anywhere close to the way he thought it would. What was it with Trin? The past two times he'd seen her she'd gone willingly into his arms and kissed him, but both times she'd told him goodbye. Not see you later or see you soon. Goodbye. Such a final word.

Zander drove back to the bed and breakfast, more depressed than he'd been in a long time. He should go crawl in bed. He hadn't had a decent night's sleep in two nights, but he was too wound up. He grabbed a sweatshirt from his room and sat on the porch swing. Not sure what he was waiting for or what he would do when it came, he waited anyway.

HARRISON RUSHED AROUND to open Trin's car door when they reached the Cloverdale. "I can see your momma raised you right," she teased.

He grinned and Trin was struck that he had grown into a very good-looking man and they'd had fun tonight, but it was just too odd to be on a date with her best friend's older brother. Moriah had such high hopes that they would hit it off, but she set them up mainly so Trin would take a break from work and "get over the fine-looking Richie."

Maybe if Trin hadn't met Zander she'd be interested in Harrison. It was pathetic that even a handsome, talented, and courteous man couldn't take her thoughts away from Zander. She hadn't even been able to enjoy *A Christmas Carol* as she replayed that dynamite kiss in her mind over and over again and the fact that Zander was back. She wanted to sing and dance rather than watch somebody do it.

"You know my momma," Harrison said. "She would kick my tail if I wasn't a gentleman."

Trin giggled because she did know his momma. As round as Moriah was thin, she kept her children in line with lots of love, laughter, and a swift smack if they ever dared mouth off.

He offered her his elbow and they walked slowly up the path to the front porch. The light was on and a shadow moved on the porch swing. Trin jumped and Harrison immediately stepped in front of her.

"Trin." Zander stood from the swing, and just looking at him made her want to melt in a puddle at his feet. How could he do this to her?

"It's okay." Trin touched Harrison's forearm which was taut like he was ready to fight. "It's my ... friend, Zander."

"Oh, yeah." Harrison nodded to Zander, but the frustration was evident in his eyes. "Nice to see you again, sir."

"You too." Zander's voice didn't leave any question that he definitely wasn't pleased to see Harrison again.

Harrison turned to Trin. "Thank you. I loved going out with you."

Trin's eyes shifted to Zander, who was glowering with his arms folded across his chest. "No, thank you. I had a wonderful time too," she said, refocusing on Harrison.

"Could we go again sometime?"

"I'd like that."

He gave her a brief hug then turned, nodded to Zander again, and walked to his beat-up Chevy sedan.

His door had barely shut and his engine fired when Zander strode across the porch and planted himself in front of Trin. "What was that? You're dating children now?"

Trin's breath puffed out in anger. "Children? Harrison is a full-grown man. If you didn't notice, I sure did."

Zander gritted his teeth and spit out, "He's a college student."

"Who is getting his master's degree because he redshirted a year and has been on scholarship for five. Plus, he's a superstar. An amazing outside linebacker for Auburn."

"Isn't that ... nice?" Zander's muscles were bunched around his neck. "I fly back from Australia as quick as I can to be with you and you're on a date."

"It's none of your business who I date and what right do you have to be waiting on my front porch like my parent?"

Zander closed his eyes and unclenched his fists. He let out a deep sigh. "Trin. I missed you. I want to be with you. Obviously you don't feel the same."

Trin took a step toward him. "Zander. I feel more for you than I've ever felt for anyone, but you left and you hardly texted and you could've been back days ago."

"You wanted me to come back?" Zander's eyes lit up and he also stepped forward.

"Of course I did. The weeks you were here were wonderful. Being with you every day."

"Are you trying to say you've fallen for me a little bit?"

"Maybe." She bit at her lip and looked at him from underneath her eyelashes. She wanted Zander, but there were still a lot of issues they needed to work through.

Zander grinned and gathered her into his arms. "Part of the reason my race was pathetic was Moriah's cookies. Most of the reason was I didn't train or race as hard because I didn't care. I wanted to be with you."

Trin trembled from his touch. She'd missed this, him, so terribly. Zander bowed his head and softly kissed her a few times. The kiss quickly became heated and he lifted her closer to him, taking full command of her mouth, her body, her every thought. He pulled away and rested his forehead against hers. "You're more addictive than any chemical, Trin."

Trin blinked and pulled back. His kisses were like a drug to her, but she suddenly knew what was wrong with their relationship and it was horrible. She stepped out of the circle of his arms and walked to the porch swing, sitting heavily.

"What's wrong?" Zander hurried to sit beside her and take her hand in his.

"Zander, me, you." Tears sprung to her eyes. "I knew something was off and I just realized what it was."

"What?" He clung to her hand.

"Have you ever heard of a co-dependent personality?"

He released her hand and leaned back against the swing. "Really,

Trin? You think I didn't hear all this crap when I was going through rehab?"

"I'm sure you did." She leaned toward him even though he was cold and closed off. "It's not crap though, Zander. I know because my stepdad is the same."

"You just compared me to your stepdad, who you don't even like?"

"Please don't get defensive and just listen to me for a minute."

"If I was attacking you, would you be defensive?"

Trin nodded. "I'm sorry. I'm not trying to attack you, but we need to figure this out because I really, truly want to be with you. Even more than I want to live here in the Cloverdale."

Zander's eyes widened. He understood what this house meant to her.

"My stepdad has been addicted to everything from smoking to golf to online gambling. When he married my mom she was his passion. I was seven and completely in the way."

"Just because you resent your stepdad doesn't mean our relationship is flawed."

"I do resent him, but there's more. He was addicted to her, madly in love, until something more shiny came along. He never cheated on her with a woman, but he's cheated on her with sports, online gaming, spending money. You name it. She's not even in the top ten things that are important to him and I've seen my younger siblings suffer as he takes a turn being obsessive about something with them then dropping them. My younger brother, Jarren, is an amazing baseball player. So for a while my stepdad was obsessed with baseball and being there for Jarren, but when Jarren didn't get picked up by a D1 school, and played at the community college instead, he dumped Jarren and hasn't been to a game since."

Zander sat completely still during her speech. Finally, he muttered, "So I remind you of your stepdad?"

"No. You're the most amazing man I know." She placed a hand on Zander's arm, praying he would understand. "I want to be with you so much I ache, but I feel like we both need to figure ourselves out before we can figure out us. Does that make sense?"

"What do you want me to do?" He stood and paced the porch. "Meet with a therapist, deal with my commitment issues, go home and come to terms with my mom's death?"

"Yes," she whispered. "I want to be here for you. I want you to forgive yourself so we can have a healthy relationship."

Zander stared at her for a few seconds and all she knew was he was angry. "If I'm like your stepdad and have only been obsessed with you because I'm co-dependent and I'm going to move on to the next 'shiny thing' why have I never, ever wanted to commit myself to a woman before this?"

Trin knew he was telling the truth and it warmed her through, but they couldn't start a relationship without him forgiving himself for his mom's death first and getting some help and her knowing she wasn't just his next "shiny thing". She stood and faced him, not afraid he would hurt her in his anger, but afraid he would leave and never come back. "I love that about you, Zander. I'm not saying we can't work, because I want you more than you'll ever know, but please, let's take some time and figure this out. I just have to know I'm not another addiction like alcohol or exercise."

Zander reared back like she'd slapped him. He studied her face like he was memorizing it then he said so quietly she almost couldn't hear him, "Maybe you should look at the fact that you're a workaholic and married to this house before you start shooting arrows."

He opened the front door and disappeared inside. Trin sank onto the porch swing, stunned, and questioning every intention she'd had. Had she just ruined everything with Zander? Had she said that all wrong? She'd become the harpie she told him she'd protect him from. The Scarlett O'Hara. Oh, that was awful. And maybe he was right about her. She hung her head, knowing she was every bit as tied to this house and taking care of it as he was training for his races. Maybe they could go talk to somebody together.

A few minutes later he returned, his arms full of luggage. He glanced at her and said, "Goodbye," then continued down the porch steps, shoved his luggage in the back of his sport utility and without another word climbed in and drove away.

"Wait," Trin whispered. She needed to explain better, needed to tell him she would try to change too, they could get help together. She finally found her legs. The car was about to pull out of the driveway. She raced down the porch steps and followed his car into the street. If he noticed, he didn't stop. She ran the entire block until his taillights were red dots and then she sank to the sidewalk. Her legs were spent and her heart was breaking. Tears streaked her cheeks as nothing but the cold cement embraced her.

CHAPTER 14

Zander couldn't get a flight out until 6:41 a.m. He wasn't surprised, both Montgomery and Burligton, Vermont were smaller airports. He slumped into a chair in terminal A5 and prepared to wait. What was one more miserable night in an airport? He heard his phone ding but didn't pull it out of his pocket. It was probably Trin and if she told him one more time that she would only love him if he saw a therapist, he was going to crack and find the nearest bar.

All the words that Trin had said and that he had thrown back at her ricocheted around in his head. She may have been right that he needed to get over his mom's death and he might need some professional help for that, but she was wrong calling him co-dependent. He went through months at Tranquility Woods and found the Lord, to give him hope, and his training, to keep him busy and productive. Plus, there was nothing wrong with being addicted to the right woman. His dad had been that way with his mom, right? He'd been a teenager when his mom died so he'd more tried to ignore them when they were loving with each other, but they'd had a great relationship.

Was Trin the right woman for him or was the cold hard truth that he hadn't allowed himself a relationship in ten years and of course the first woman he let in would be amazing? He slumped down in the vinyl chair, ignoring the lady three seats down chatting away on her cell phone. Who was she talking to at midnight anyway? An announcement came that Flight 1541 to Atlanta was now boarding.

Zander closed his eyes and pictured Trin. If she were any more right for him, she would've had to be hand-delivered to him by angels. Maybe his mom had a part in them coming together. He groaned. Why couldn't she accept him as he was? Why did she always throw up another barrier between them?

Yet, he was right about the fact that she was a workaholic. Would she leave her house for him? Could he ask that of her? Yes, if they ever wanted to have a life together. Working with her at the Cloverdale had been enjoyable, mostly because he was with her, but also because he had a purpose. Maybe she was right and he did need to do more with his means and influence, but he didn't want to be tied to something the way she was. He laid his head back on the seat and wished the time would go faster. The longer he sat here the more he wanted to grab another rental car and go back to Trin. He couldn't do that. He was going home. That was enough of a sacrifice for right now. He dreaded seeing his childhood home, but was excited at the same time. If only things were right with him and Trin. Having her with him would make it so much easier.

Zander flew into Burlington and rented a car. The drive to Essex Junction was too short, but he couldn't get enough of the familiar sites around him. The leaves had fallen, but he still thought his home state was the prettiest around. Why had he let so much time go by since he'd come here? The rolling hills passed quickly and before he knew it he was pulling into his father's estate. He gripped the steering wheel with both hands and his neck muscles needed a highly trained masseuse.

The guard waiting at the gate was unfamiliar to him. "Can I help you, sir?"

"Yes. I'm …" He cleared his throat and forced out the words. "Zander Keller. Here to see my father."

"Welcome, sir." The guard's reluctant expression changed to open inspection. He must've seen the family resemblance as he didn't ask for ID. The gate automatically swung wide. Zander eased the rental car through. His hands trembled against the steering wheel so he clutched it tighter, making his neck ache more. He stared around at the wooded property. This time of year with the leaves gone, he could actually see through the thick forest, but mostly there were just more trees to see. The lake where he had swum as a child and teenager was barely visible.

He pulled around the circle drive, put the car in park, and rested his head on the steering wheel. Could he go in that house? Knowing his mom would not be there to greet him? Maybe it was pathetic of him, but it was the reason he'd never come back. His dad had somehow understood that Zander couldn't face the house without her and had allowed him to stay at a hotel until the funeral was over then go to a boarding school in upstate New York for his senior year. Distancing himself from everything that reminded him of his mom, including his dad was the only way he'd survived. Well, that and the alcohol.

His car door popped open and Zander jerked up. His dad stood there, beaming. "My boy." He choked up and couldn't say anymore, but tugged on Zander's arm. Zander allowed himself to be pulled from the car and into his father's arms. He was taller than his dad, but he rested his head on his shoulder and let the tears come.

"You're home," his dad kept saying, "You're really home."

Zander finally pulled himself together and straightened up. "It was time," he muttered.

"I'm so happy." His dad scrubbed the tears from his own face.

"He's here!" The shriek came from the front steps.

Zander whirled and dang it if the tears didn't start up again. "Hannah!" He raced up the stairs and lifted the little woman into his arms, swinging her around.

She giggled and swatted at him. "Put me down, you handsome thing you, I ain't as young as I used to be."

Her red hair did have some streaks of gray, but she still had a sparkle in her blue eyes. He'd seen her almost every Christmas, but coming home made him take more notice of the changes.

"I missed you." He set her on her feet, but kept one arm around her.

His dad joined them on the porch, grinning at both of them.

"You better have missed my cooking as much as you missed me. Look at you—all muscle and bone. I'd better get to whipping up some of your favorite creamy chicken potato soup with homemade bread and honey butter. Why didn't you tell us you were coming so I could have it all ready?"

"Sorry." Zander shrugged.

"No worries. You talk with your father then you come chat with me while I cook. I'll put you to work like I used to."

"Sounds good." Zander would rather go work in the kitchen than have the heart-to-heart with his father he'd been putting off for ten years.

Hannah scurried away. Zander glanced around the yard. "It's weird to not have Mr. Tyler here."

"Yeah. I miss Horace a lot."

Even though he'd adored the old man, he couldn't recall ever hearing his first name. It was always Mr. Tyler.

"It's been five years," his dad said. "Crazy how time flies."

"No. I thought it was just a couple years ago." Zander stopped at the front door and focused on his dad. It was easier than walking through the threshold right now.

"No, five."

Zander had lost out on a lot, drinking his life away. He felt Mr. Tyler's loss anew being home and not having him here. He slowly digested it. "Was it old age that took him?"

"Cancer. He was only seventy-two when he passed."

Zander nodded. Death was not something he dealt with, at all.

His father gestured for him to go ahead. Zander took a deep

breath. He'd competed in eleven Ironmans over the past two years. He could do this. He could walk into his childhood home. He steeled his spine and took a long stride, hurrying over the step and into the foyer. The paint was lighter, but the chandelier was the same. He couldn't stop himself from looking around the spacious foyer, up the sweeping staircase, hoping beyond hope that maybe her ghost would at least sweep down and greet him. He closed his eyes and tried to shake some sense into his head.

His dad grasped his arm. "You okay?" He alone knew what this cost Zander. Everyone but his dad and Hannah had dropped away in his life. He hadn't realized how alone he was and that he really didn't want to be alone, until Trin had come into his life. Now she was gone and he wasn't sure why he thought coming home would be a good idea. The pain of Trin's loss and the pain of dealing with his mom's death. He was really glutton for pain today.

"It's not as bad as I feared." The lie was easier than the truth.

His dad gave him an encouraging smile and led him to the left to the music room, her room. Zander wanted to dig his heels in and throw a childhood fit. He marched stoically next to his dad, trying to lock his heart and avoid the anguish.

His dad eased the door open and swung it wide. Zander swore he could hear someone plucking at the harp. His mom's harp. He took a tentative step into the room. Late afternoon sunlight streamed through the floor to ceiling windows. The highly-polished instruments all stood in their appointed spots—piano, organ, harp, and Zander's old drum set. He turned to his dad and surprised himself by laughing. "You keep my drums in here still?"

"Remember how you loved to play and accompany her?"

"She was so patient with me." Zander pushed a hand through his hair. "I made her music sound horrible and she never once told me no."

"She thought you were the greatest person to ever live," his dad murmured.

Zander knew it wasn't an exaggeration. He could never do any wrong in his mother's eyes. He blinked quickly and looked at the harp. Her favorite instrument. Drawn to it, he found himself walking over and plucking a few strings. The soft sound floated up to him. Zander wrapped his hand around the frame. He didn't realize he was crying until the tears splattered against the gold paint.

Sinking into the chair he'd often found his mother in, he took a few quick breaths. He needed to calm down, needed to get in control. His dad bent down and wrapped his arms around him. "Let it out, son. It's okay. It's been ten years. I think you deserve to let it go."

Zander's entire body trembled as he released sorrow he'd buried. He stood and turned into his dad's embrace. "I'm so sorry, Dad," he sobbed. "I'm sorry I didn't protect her."

His dad pulled back and shook him gently by both shoulders. "Oh, son. It wasn't your fault. It was mine. I went to that conference instead of being there for both of you. Please, please don't blame yourself."

Zander shook his head and sniffled. "Dad. I was the one that should've been there. I went to a bonfire and chased girls then I went drinking with the other football players. You can't blame yourself."

His dad shook his head and gave a strangled laugh. "I thought you blamed me. I thought that's why you never came home."

"Oh, no." Zander exhaled and almost stopped the torrent of tears. "Dad, I couldn't come home without her here. It was all my fault. I'd ruined our family and I couldn't face it."

His dad stared at him. "Oh, my boy." He pulled him against his chest again and his tears wet Zander's shirt. "It's time to forgive yourself. I've never blamed you. You were a child." He took a long breath. "Can you please forgive me, son?"

Zander nodded against the soft material of his dad's cotton shirt. "Yes, Dad. I never blamed you either."

His dad wrapped an arm around his shoulder and led him out of the music room. They went across the entryway to his dad's office and sat side by side in plush chairs. His dad kept a hand on Zander's arm like he wasn't ready to disconnect yet.

"I went to a psychiatrist the year after I lost her," his dad admitted. "It helped a lot. I still stop by sometimes when the guilt gets to be too much."

Zander's fists clenched. Was his dad going to suggest what everyone did?

"Would you go visit with her? For me?"

There it was, and how did you tell the man who gave you everything, and who didn't blame you for his wife's death, no. Trin wanted him to go meet with someone. The two people he loved the most thought he needed help. Maybe he did.

"I'll try it, Dad."

"Thank you." His dad squeezed his arm. "What else is going on? How's Trin?"

Zander looked out the windows at the bare forest. "She's amazing and hard-working and pretty ticked at me right now."

His dad surprised him by releasing his arm and laughing.

"What?" Zander sat up straighter. His dad's laughter warmed him, but he was confused by the sudden change.

"So my plan worked."

"What plan?" Zander leaned closer, staring into his dad's blue eyes. He realized he was looking more like his father every day.

"You're a smart boy, Zander. Did you really think I was worried about Trin's work ethic or the profitability of a small bed and breakfast that has no debt and is almost always booked?"

"I wondered, but I just did what you asked me to do."

"You've always done that."

Zander studied his dad. "You've been pretty understanding, Dad."

"That's what you do when you love someone as much as I love you."

Zander smiled, fighting at more tears. "So, why did you send me to Montgomery?"

"Trin." His dad said simply.

"You conniving father." Zander sat back, awareness shooting through him. "You wanted me to get together with Trin."

"I hoped you could learn something from her dedication to the Cloverdale. She's grounded in a way I thought would draw you in. And you're right, I was hoping you'd see what an amazing woman she is." He grinned. "I feel like she could be the one for you. Like your mother was for me."

There was no good reply for that, especially with how he left Trin last night, or was it early this morning? "Would you ever remarry, Dad?"

He smiled, removed his hand from Zander's arms and folded his hands together. "Well, son, now that you're here I'd like to ask your permission."

"Permission?"

"To marry Hannah. These past few years I've realized how much she's come to mean to me. She's agreed to marry me, but we wanted your approval first. She said if you came home it would be the sign that we should marry."

"No wonder she was so happy to see me."

His dad chuckled. "She'd be thrilled to see you no matter what. You know that."

Zander did. His dad and Hannah. It made sense. Hannah's husband had died young and she'd raised a couple of boys who were years older than Zander on her own before coming to work for the family. He hated to think about his mom being replaced, but ten years was a long time to be alone. His dad deserved happiness, and he couldn't think of anyone he'd rather have him with than Hannah.

"You need to go see Trin," his dad interrupted his thoughts.

"I can't, Dad. I made a huge fool of myself and she was with a great guy last night." He shook his head, remembering Moriah's brother stepping in front of Trin to protect her when Zander had been waiting for them on the porch. He'd heard Harrison ask her out again and she'd agreed. "It's too late."

"It's never too late, son. Don't miss out on a minute of being with her. I'll never regret any time I had with your mother."

"Dad." He paused and studied his hands. "Trin claims I'm an addictive personality, called me co-dependent. She wanted me to figure things out before I try to be with her." He sighed. "It made me mad that she thought she could psychoanalyze me, so I told her off and left."

His dad reclined into his chair. "I think we're both that type of personality, son. I did everything for your mother in the hopes that she would spend every spare minute with me. I was obsessive about her. The psychiatrist really helped me recognize that and acknowledge that I do it in a lot of areas of my life—work for example."

Zander didn't love the words he was hearing. "I went through all that therapy to overcome alcohol. I thought that was enough."

"Maybe it was, but there's nothing wrong with getting some help. It's just tough to admit you're struggling."

Zander snickered. "I think anyone who knows me would recognize I'm struggling. I've been a mess for the past ten years."

His dad nodded in commiseration. "I'm right there with you."

Zander knew his dad was. He was thrilled that he could find happiness with Hannah.

"Isn't Trin worth trying to work through the issues?"

"You know she is."

His dad stood. "Let's go help Hannah in the kitchen. I'll make an appointment with the psychiatrist for tomorrow if you'd like."

"Okay." He stood and they walked arm in arm through the house. It hurt to be home, but it felt great too. When Hannah threw her arms around him again and then gave him a pinch of cookie dough, he savored the tastes, smells, and the glances he caught between Hannah and his dad. He couldn't believe it'd taken him so long to get here, but it was the best therapy he could imagine.

CHAPTER 15

Trin stayed busy throughout the month of December. She trained two new front office girls, a housekeeper, and a groundskeeper. Moriah was able to focus on the baking and cooking like she loved, and Trin made her assistant manager. With her new raise, Moriah spent a lot more time with Turk and was putting away money for a down payment on their own little house. She was thrilled.

Trin had met with a counselor at the nearby Baptist church and started working through her resentment to her mom and stepdad, and her security issues that made her think she had to work every minute of the day so she could keep her grandparents' house. It was amazing how turning it over to the Lord had helped. She didn't know if she could've done it on her own. Having faith was new, but so worth it.

She was trying to take time for herself more also. She'd found a friend at Moriah's church who loved tennis and they played several times a week. She'd also taken up running, trying to convince herself it wasn't because of the connection she felt to Zander when she ran, knowing he loved it and he'd run all of these streets when he was here in November.

She hadn't heard from him. His dad's communication was positive and inspiring as ever, but he didn't say anything about Zander. Trin wondered where he was, what he was doing. Training for another race, most likely.

Christmas Day was rainy, but after she talked to her mom and siblings, heard all about their Christmas, and thanked them for their presents, she dressed in a t-shirt and fitted running pants and laced up her shoes. She was going to dinner at Moriah's house later; she hoped things wouldn't be awkward with Harrison. She'd told him no when he asked her out a couple of days ago. He was one of the best young men she knew, but he wasn't Zander.

She had the morning all to herself. They'd blocked out a couple days before and after Christmas to have no guests at the bed and breakfast. They were booked up again three days after Christmas, but it was nice to have things quiet today. The house could easily have filled for the holidays, but Mr. Keller had reminded her that the Cloverdale was in the black and it was okay to not work all the time.

Trin jogged through the quiet, wet streets. It seemed almost other-worldly with the sun breaking through the clouds in the distance, but drizzle falling all around her. She went a few miles then turned back home. As she neared the bed and breakfast, she noticed a black Mercedes in the driveway. She resented someone interrupting her solitude this morning. She wanted to think about Christmas, the Savior, and how much she missed Zander, not have to turn away a guest who should've made travel plans much earlier than Christmas Day.

The car door popped open when she was still a couple of houses away. Trin squinted as long, lean legs swung out of the door, followed by a muscular frame and handsome face she would recognize anywhere.

"Zander!" she screamed, sprinting across the distance, splashing through a huge puddle and soaking her legs.

He turned and that irresistible grin split his face. Trin slammed into him. Zander picked her off her feet and kissed her. She clung to him, the wetness from the rain intermingling with the sweet taste of

Zander. He released her from the kiss, chuckled, and held her close to him.

"You're soaking wet," he said.

"Who cares? You're here!"

"You wanted me here?"

"Yes!" She squeezed his broad back. "Where did you think I wanted you?"

"In therapy." He laughed.

"I wanted you to get some help, that did not mean I wanted you to desert me."

He laughed again. The water streamed down his face. His hair was dripping and Trin was certain no man had ever been more handsome.

"I went home and I got therapy, renewed my faith in the Lord too. My dad, Hannah, my house, and our pastor, helped as much as the psychiatrist."

Trin wasn't sure if the moisture running down her face was more from rain or tears. "I'm so proud of you. I've been meeting with someone too. I'm trying to find a balance between work and life. Trying to have more faith that everything will work out and my grandparents' memory will still be with me, even if I'm not here at the house."

"Oh, Trin." He swept her off her feet and carried her up the porch steps. Setting her down under the overhang where they wouldn't be pounded by the rain, he stared at her and gently traced a finger across her cheek. Trin trembled from his touch and wanted more than anything to kiss him again.

"I have a proposition for you."

"Lay it on me."

He grinned. "I want to start a foundation that helps children— foster children, those with single parents, or those with parents who are struggling financially. I'm going to organize triathlons and Iron-mans and use all the revenue to help. Plus, twenty percent of my sales from my products will go to the foundation. I'm calling it, Moriah's Munchkins."

"Oh, she'll love that!" Trin loved it too. The purpose it would mean for him, but what did this mean for her, for them? At least she was still in his arms.

"I know you love the Cloverdale. What if I bought a mansion near here for us to live, and you could still manage the bed and breakfast while I manage my organization? But you have to agree to only be an assistant manager, promote Moriah to manager, and be willing to travel with me and take entire weeks off to be with me."

She inclined her head. "Are you saying …?"

"Yes, love." He took both of her hands in his and squeezed them. "I know this is probably too quick for you, but I love you, Trin Dean. I love you and I am miserable without you. Will you marry me?"

Trin smiled so big her cheeks hurt. "I love you too, Jason Hunley."

Zander threw back his head and laughed. He wrapped his warm hands around her face and lowered his head to hers. "Say my name, please, love."

"Zander Keller. The man who has my heart."

"Oh, that was cheesy. I love it." Zander pressed his lips to hers and Trin clung to him. Wet, but not alone. Never alone again.

ABOUT THE AUTHOR

Cami is a part-time author, part-time exercise consultant, part-time housekeeper, full-time wife, and overtime mother of four adorable boys. Sleep and relaxation are fond memories. She's never been happier.

Sign up for Cami's newsletter to receive a free ebook copy of *The Feisty One: A Billionaire Bride Pact Romance* and information about new releases, discounts, and promotions here.

If you enjoyed *The Faithful One,* please consider posting a review on Amazon, Goodreads, or your personal blog. Thank you for helping to spread the word.

www.camichecketts.com
cami@camichecketts.com

ALSO BY CAMI CHECKETTS

THE ADVENTUROUS ONE BY JEANETTE LEWIS

"What's ahead for you?" Taylor asked as they sat on the restaurant patio with sandwiches and salads. They were at a small round table and had pulled their chairs so close they were almost touching. The sun was warm on their faces and a small breeze ruffled their hair. Taylor thought of the skydiving and wanted to go back.

Lane picked at his pasta salad with his fork. "I don't know. Same old, same old I guess. Work. What about you?"

Her face fell. "I'm not sure. I mean, I submit my travel plans to my editor a year in advance, so I guess I'll be picking up where I left off in my schedule when I leave here. I just ..." She trailed off, unsure how to phrase it.

"You're wondering what's ahead for us?" he asked softly.

Heart in her throat, she nodded. The differences between this day with Lane and the day on the boat with Brent were stark in her mind. No guilt, no harsh words, no second guessing, no nerves—except for the good kind. Just being with him, just looking at him, sent thrills shooting through her core and goosebumps parading up her arms. It was embarrassing, really, though if he'd noticed, he hadn't commented.

Lane put his fork down and reached for her hand. His fingers closed around hers, warm and strong. "I don't know," he admitted. "I really like you. No, scratch that, I more than like you."

Taylor gave up all pretense of playing it cool. "I more than like you too," she whispered.

He flashed her a smile, then he was leaning toward her and she was leaning toward him. There was a moment, right before she closed her eyes, when she could see the flecks of gold in his hazel eyes, the fringe of lashes around them. He smelled clean and soapy and faintly like pine trees. Then her eyes fluttered closed and his lips brushed hers, warm and soft.

She didn't remember dropping her fork, but suddenly her hands were free, sliding up the warm contours of his arms, over his muscular shoulders, and into the thick hair at the back of his head. Heat and longing exploded through her body as she wound her fingers into his hair as his mouth claimed hers. He tasted like cola and salad dressing, like spending a lazy summer day in a hammock, like swimming in a warm hot springs, like freedom and passion and love.

Lane's arms were around her, one clamped at her waist, the other at the back of neck, guiding her head so their mouths moved in sync.

"Get a room!" Someone hollered, another diner on the patio, and they broke apart. For a moment they stared at each other, unsure whether to be embarrassed by so much PDA, but then Taylor giggled. She didn't care.

Lane laughed. "Sorry about that," he called to the person who yelled. "Can you blame me though?"

The man chuckled, shaking his head, and went back to his lunch.

"Wow," Lane leaned forward, resting his forehead against Taylor's. "Can we do that again?"

She couldn't quite catch her breath. "Come with me," she whispered, before she could think.

His eyes grew big. "What do you mean?"

It was pure impulse, brought on by desire and raging hormones, but more than that, the knowledge that *this* was what she'd wanted from the moment she'd seen him again. She wanted to explore the world with this man at her side. "No expectations," she added quickly, seeing the confusion in his eyes. "We'd get separate rooms, like when Summer and I travel with her boyfriends. I just ... I think it would be really fun to have you along, and I think you'd like it. It could be the way it was, at the outdoor club, the two of us, together. I want you to come, *need* you to come ... need you," she finished shakily.

He ran one hand down the curve of her cheek and sat back. "What's your next trip?" He asked.

"I cut my trip to Mexico short to come help with Grandma, so I have a couple more weeks free, but then in August, I start the Appalachian Trail." The thought of having Lane along turned it from an exciting hike into a magical adventure.

"The Appalachian Trail is over two thousand miles long," Lane said. "You're hiking *all* of it?"

"Not the whole thing," she said. "I haven't finalized my route yet, but I'm planning to be in New England by autumn to see the leaves. Depending on how much longer Grandma needs me, I might start there and work my way south. What do you think?"

She'd thought it would be exactly like the kind of thing Lane would love. But his face fell and he stared past her at their reflection in the restaurant windows. "Yeah, sounds great," he said slowly. "If I could walk more than a mile without needing to rest. Or if I could even get up an incline as steep as a dopey bridge in a city park."

"So that's where my friend comes in," Taylor urged. "She can help you get the equipment you need so you *can* do that kind of stuff, don't you see?" Her palms were clammy—please let him say yes. Please let him see this was possible.

But Lane shook his head and poked at his salad again with his fork. "I can't," he muttered. "I can't take charity."

Taylor groaned in frustration. "Will you shelve your silly pride for a few minutes," she urged.

It was the wrong thing to say. Lane's head shot up and his eyes turned cold. "My *pride* is what got me through," he said quietly. "It's about the only thing I have left."

"But it doesn't have to be that way," she said, on a roll now that she couldn't stop, didn't want to stop. "You don't have to just accept this is the way your life is now, there are still lots of things you could be doing, lots of adventures you could be having, if you'll let yourself."

"I'll get there, Taylor," he said firmly. "But on my own terms."

She shook her head, tears brimming in her eyes. "No you won't. You'll go on working in your stupid little office and struggling along and never doing anything you've dreamed about because you're too stubborn to realize someone tried to give you exactly what you needed and you refused."

His hand clenched around his fork. "You have no idea what it's like," he grated.

"You're right, I don't. What you've been through is beyond imagining and I have no frame of reference for it. But I do know what it's like to be hurt ... so devastated that you think you're beyond repair. I've been there, and it took a long time, but I learned you can't let one terrible thing define you for the rest of your life."

"It's not the same," he insisted. "You didn't lose a third of your body."

"That's true," Taylor said carefully, sensing dangerous territory. "Something horrendous happened to you, more awful than I can even imagine. But you're more than your legs, you're more than one day, one decision, one tragic accident. You have all kinds of things about you that have nothing to do with any of that, but you're ignoring all the good things to focus only on this one bad thing." She put her hand on his arm, trying to soften the words. "You can pay her back if that's what you're worried about, but don't waste these best years of your life. Once they're gone, they're gone. Money is a renewable commodity, but time isn't."

His Adam's apple bobbed as he swallowed hard, looking as if he was on the verge of tears, just as she was.

"Please?" she whispered.

He shook his head. "I can't."

Read more or buy *The Adventurous One* here.

PASS INTERFERENCE: A LAST PLAY ROMANCE BY CAMI CHECKETTS

"Lily." Ike interrupted her as she demonstrated to the six a.m. group training session how to do a proper dropping pushup. Several of them were cheating and she knew they could do it correctly and would thank, or possibly cuss, her tomorrow when their chest muscles felt like they'd been ripped apart.

"Malee needs you," Ike said.

"I'm in the middle of a session here."

"I'll take over."

She hesitated.

"She said it's really important." Ike winked. "Like maybe as important as you going out with me Saturday night."

"Not happening, Ike."

Several of the class members overheard and snickered at Lily shooting down the body-building trainer. His looks weren't the problem, it was his attitude toward women. Like they were beneath him in the professional realm, but he would forgive them for that if they fawned all over him and dated him. Ick. He asked Lily out so often she'd become an expert at rejecting him.

"You'll give in someday."

She laughed. "I highly doubt that."

"You really need to go talk to Malee now."

Lily noted that he was actually being serious and acquiesced. "Okay. The workout's all on the board."

Ike squeezed her arm as she walked past.

"Thanks," she muttered. He was an okay guy, but always too cocky and flirtatious. She was at the gym to work or workout, not to flirt, but that was a hard concept for some of the men.

A few of her class participants gave her desperate looks. They liked her to be there to motivate them through the boot camp style class. Ike did a good job. He just wasn't as intense as she was, tended to start talking with the clients rather than pushing and motivating them the entire hour.

Lily always made sure that her clients got their money and time's worth and then some. She'd lived through lean times growing up with six siblings and fighting her way through college with a scholarship, grants, and a full-time waitressing job. She worked in the fanciest gym in Golden, Colorado, the Fitness Academy. It was nice and had all the equipment a trainer or gym goer could hope for. It might not be as ritzy as some of the gyms in downtown Denver, but it was closer to her home and family in Georgetown, and the rent in Golden was much cheaper than Denver. Some trainers, Ike, would claim she shouldn't feel guilty about taking rich people's money, but she refused to take advantage of a client's time or money, no matter how much of it they seemed to have.

She walked down the hallway and the stairs to the personal training office across from the main weight room. Poking her head in, she saw a tall, well-formed man with his back to her. Some men were just built right and this guy definitely had some good genes. The broad shoulders and sculpted lines of his neck, back, and arms, right down to his glutes and legs. The soft cotton of his T-shirt and fleece of his sweats couldn't hide any of his musculature from her trained eye.

Was he applying to be a new trainer? Lily immediately felt the competition swell in her. She was fighting to get enough clients as it was. Giving deals for training and trying to prove she was every bit as good as any male trainer. With her specialty in sports-specific training, she was building up a great clientele of high school athletes, and even some from the local college. Her dream was to someday work for the Denver Storm. A girl had to have dreams, even if they were monstrously big.

Her boss, Malee, stared at the man as if he was a superstar. That didn't bode well if she was hiring him to train here. Lily really liked Malee and she was great to shuttle clients Lily's way, but this guy could steal her clientele just by being a walking billboard. Maybe he was a future client, though he didn't look like he needed any body sculpting help, that was for sure. Their low conversation didn't carry, so sadly Lily wasn't getting any clues ahead of time.

Lily stepped into the office all the way. Malee's head popped up and the man turned to face her. Lily's jaw dropped. That good-looking face was not one anybody who had an electronic device of any kind wouldn't recognize. "You're, holy Toledo, you're Hyde Metcalf!"

He smiled and she honestly wanted to swoon right then and there. "Holy Toledo?"

She blushed.

On camera, Hyde Metcalf always seemed to have half a smile on his face, like he knew a joke everybody wanted to be privy to. But when he really smiled, wow, it was a good one. She didn't have as much insight as she wanted to about his personal life because she tried diligently not to become obsessive about him, but she knew he had an African American father who'd also played for the Storm back in his day and a beautiful, blonde mother. He was the perfect blend of his parents. His eyes were dark with long lashes framing them and his face was just nice—the right amount of manly lines with enough softness to make him real.

Just because she didn't allow herself to Google his personal life any more than once a week, or read every article put out by the gossip magazines about him, didn't mean she didn't know his every stat, watch his games faithfully, and follow him on Twitter, Instagram,

Facebook, really wherever he had an account. Okay, she was pathetically star struck by him.

Her hands were trembling with nervous excitement and she wasn't sure what her face was doing. She wanted to touch him and make sure he was real.

"And I hear you're Lily Udy," Hyde said, extending his hand to shake hers.

"The one and only." Lily gave him a firm handshake, liking the size of his hands. Of course they had to be big to snatch the ball out of the air like he did. Oh, my, goodness, he was real. She wanted to jump up and down, take a selfie with him, and call her brothers to tell them how amazing this was—she was meeting Hyde Metcalf and he knew *her* name. Her youngest brother, Josh, would go completely berserk.

"Malee is telling me you're the best sports specific trainer in Golden," he said.

Lily cocked her head and tried to appear confident, though he could probably see the pulse in her neck jumping. "Maybe in the state of Colorado."

He chuckled. "Oh, I like confidence. This is the girl I need."

Need for what? Because she was totally up for whatever he needed. *Lily!* Her mother's voice in her head told her not to be infatuated with him just because the guy was a big time star. But come on, she loved him. Well, not loved him, loved him, but he was the best wide receiver to play the game. He had 1871 receiving yards last year. Plus, he was always just doing cool things. Coordinating an event to raise money for juvenile diabetes research and, from the video footage she saw, spending time with many of the children one on one. Helping a single mom whose daughter had cancer with medical bills. The media captured all of it and she knew famous people had a hard time hiding nowadays.

The only bad media he got was when his mother was interviewed, an older blonde lady who was a bit rotund, but still beautiful. It was interesting that they involved his mom so much, but she always said hilarious things, usually bragging about her "sweet, little boy", but she always seemed to somehow cut his girlfriends down and whether it was intentional or not, it came out pretty funny, but not exactly good PR. The other day she'd told a reporter, "That girl's shorts were so short I saw her tush." The reporter had goaded her and she'd continued with, "Well, I shouldn't say the word tramp, but if *you* saw her tush what would you think?" Last year, she'd called one of his girlfriends a "floozie" then she'd been horrified when the reporter looked shocked and she kept repeating, "I meant frou-frou because she dresses so ... fancy all the time." The press had a field day laughing about that one.

Okay, so maybe she Googled Hyde more often than once a week and knew a few things about his personal life.

"Hyde wanted to meet you before we signed the contract," Malee said.

"Contract?" *Oh my, calm down, heart. Hyde Metcalf is looking at me and smiling!*

"You probably heard about the pneumonia?" Hyde asked.

"Follow you on Twitter," she admitted.

"Nice. I like a girl who's informed." He cocked an eyebrow and folded those beautiful arms across his chest. Yum, what she wouldn't do to work with biceps like that, or touch them, touching them would be a little creepy though, right?

"I've recently been cleared to return to physical activity," Hyde was saying and she tried to keep up, "and I've got two months until practice starts full bore for the season. I'd like you to train me."

Lily had to grab onto a nearby chair. "Your team trainers are some of the best in the nation."

"Hey, what happened to that confidence?" He cocked an eyebrow at her. "You're the best in the state of Colorado."

"I am. But I'm a year out of college, I don't have the experience your trainers have." She had to be honest with him, even if it killed her if he decided to walk away.

"So you should have all the most recent training info," Hyde said.

Lily gave him a grateful smile and tried to find that confidence again. She was a specialist in sports training and she could do this. She could do a fabulous job of training this man to be ready for the season, but truly he did have some amazing trainers at his disposal.

"Yes, that's right," she said, "but why did you choose our gym?" *Shut up, Lily, and sign the stinking contract before he gets away.*

"I wanted to stay close to home," Hyde admitted, ducking his head.

Lily raised her eyebrows, waiting for him to explain. She knew he was from Golden, everyone in the town knew and were more proud of that fact than Livability.com listing Golden as a top small town. But Hyde didn't live here anymore, did he? She tried to remember all the places he had homes—a coastal place in California, some island in the Caribbean, and maybe Park City, Utah. She'd have to check, but he also had a penthouse in downtown Denver. I mean, come on, the man made over fourteen million dollars a year and who knew how much in endorsements? Who wouldn't want that face selling cologne on television? She'd buy whatever he sold, if she could afford it.

"My mom needed some help so I had her house remodeled a few months back and I'm staying with her."

Whoa. He obviously didn't need to share that information with two basically strangers. She could see why he kept it on the down low. The press would have a heyday with the mega-stud moving back in with Mom, no matter what the reason.

"That's so sweet," Malee gushed.

Lily stared at her friend. It was sweet and Malee was obviously as infatuated with him as Lily was. Lily couldn't blame her.

"I wanted a trainer and gym close by so I don't have to drive into Denver every day for workouts until practice and team training officially start. My agent got great recommendations for The Fitness Academy."

Lily nodded. "Well, you made a good choice."

He smiled again, looking relieved. "I hope so." He sobered. "But you really do have to be the best. I'll give you one week to prove yourself. If I'm satisfied with your workouts and my progress, I'll keep working with you and give you a ten thousand dollar bonus at the end of June. If I'm not satisfied, I'll pay off the training for May, but I'll have to go with the team trainers."

Lily gulped. A ten thousand dollar bonus? Oh, she loved this guy so much.

"Malee informed me that your hourly rate is a hundred. That's reasonable."

A hundred? She charged sixty at the very most, quite often less, and usually was doing package deals where her clients got an hour free for every three hours they trained. Malee was giving her the glare, telling her not to reveal any of what she was thinking. Lily's breath caught. Tick off her boss and maybe lose her dream client or be honest?

"I don't usually charge that much," she said in a rush.

Hyde looked her over and nodded. "That's okay. I'll pay a hundred."

Lily exhaled, grateful she'd spoken up and even more grateful he'd dealt with her revelation so well.

"I'd like to do two hours a day, six days a week," Hyde continued.

Lily appreciated that he was a get things done kind of a guy, but seemed like he could joke and make things fun as well. He was every bit as cool as his media persona, maybe more, and she got to train him for two hours a day, six days a week, for the next two months. Her brothers were going to be insane with jealousy. Her little brothers idolized Hyde Metcalf, especially the youngest, Josh. She wondered if there was any way she could arrange a meeting. It would be the highlight of Josh's life.

"When do you want to start?" she asked.

"Right now."

"You're cleared for all activity?" She was already planning the workout she'd put him through.

"Malee has the doc's note."

She put out her hand and grinned. "Let's do it."

He stepped closer and grasped her hand again, but this time it wasn't a nice to meet you handshake, more like—you passed the test and now you get the privilege of shaking my hand good and long. Lily noticed that his hands were not only big, but tingly. Wait, were they tingly or was she? The scent of fabric softener and musky man smell wafted over her.

"Snuggle?" she asked.

"Excuse me?"

"Do you use Snuggle fabric softener?"

He laughed. "I think so. My mom insists on doing the laundry rather than sending it out."

He came from a different world than her obviously, and she wondered what the media would do to him when they found out he was living with his mom again. The momma's boy taunts would probably be horrid, but she thought it was pretty honorable. Moving back home to take care of his mom. She wondered what was wrong with his mom and she wondered if she needed to let go of his hand now.

She forced herself to release the clasp and he looked down quickly, as if he wasn't ready to be done touching her either. Okay. She had to keep this professional no matter how smitten she was. This was a huge paycheck for her and the gym, and also a huge advertising tool. She could imagine Malee was planning all kinds of scoops on that one.

"Obviously people are going to know I'm coming here, but I'd like you to wait on using me for advertising until after July first." He looked at Malee. "Can you add that to the contract?"

Malee nodded, sat at her computer and typed away.

"We have a private room upstairs where we do personal training," Lily said. "If you're okay with seven to nine in the morning or any time between eleven and four we could workout in there and not many people would see you."

"Do you have all the equipment we need?"

"Yes, or I'll bring it in from the main weight room. I'd also like to do some workouts outside."

His smile crinkled his cheeks. "I'd like that too. Let's go for the morning time slot."

Malee pulled the printed pages from the copier. "Can you look this over, Mr. Metcalf, then sign at the bottom. I'll also need a credit card for billing purposes."

"I'm going to run quick and check on my class while you sign the paperwork," Lily said. "They should be finishing up, but I don't want them to think I left them hanging."

"Okay." Hyde nodded to her.

Lily bounced upstairs and down the hallway. She could not believe this blessing that had fallen from heaven. She wanted to scream and dance, but forced herself to be somewhat calm.

Ike was talking to a couple of the girls from her class, but everyone else was gone. "Are they already done?" she asked.

"I let them out early for good behavior." Ike winked. "I'd do more than that for you if you could demonstrate a little good behavior."

Lily glared at him. "Stop, Ike."

The girls giggled and said their goodbyes as Ike strode right up to her.

She stood her ground, not willing to back away and let him think he could bully her. "I don't like you making my class too easy," she said.

"I could make things real easy with you." Ike had the nerve to brush his fingers up her arm.

Lily whirled from him and ran right into Hyde Metcalf. Hyde held onto her arms to steady her and she was amazed at the difference of his solid, entrancing touch and Ike's touch that felt like creepy spiders on her skin.

"You okay?" Hyde asked in a low tone. He lifted his eyes over her head and pinned them on Ike.

"Yes, I'm fine."

Ike smirked as he walked around them. If he knew who Hyde was, he didn't acknowledge it. "See you later, sweetheart," Ike said to Lily.

Lily ignored him, trying to hide the shudder that ran through her. She didn't want to be unprofessional with Hyde watching.

Hyde kept his eyes on Ike until the trainer rounded the corner then he turned back to Lily.

"You ready?" she asked.

"Sure." He grinned at her. "Put me to work."

Lily rubbed her hands together, putting Ike completely from her mind. She was training Hyde Metcalf. Super athlete extraordinaire. It was better than being a Denver Storm trainer. She got Hyde one-on-one and this paycheck was going to make a huge difference for her family, especially her sister just younger than her. Life had just taken an enormous upswing.

Find Pass Interference on Amazon.

THE CHRISTMAS GROOM BY
TAYLOR HART

The Christmas Groom

By Taylor Hart

Chapter 1

Nathan Pennington sank low into his ski boots and breathed in the cool Park City mountain air. It'd been a rough three months.

His father had died right before the election they'd been planning for two years. Granted, he still had a law firm to run he'd inherited from his father. He also had several oil companies and a plethora of businesses his father had owned. His movie star brother, Sterling, wanted nothing to do with them.

But the businesses didn't replace the loneliness growing inside of him. He often told himself it would get better. After all, he was closer to his brother then he'd ever been. Which was nice.

But, he missed his father. He missed...being so wrapped up in his father's affairs, he didn't have time to hardly think about the lack of relationships in his own life.

Until now.

When the calendar had flipped to December first, though, something had changed inside of him. It was as if he suddenly noticed something was lacking in his life. He was twenty-eight years old and had never been married—hardly even had a relationship, even if he counted the two-year thing during law school.

All month long he'd been "squirmy," as his secretary had called it, and she told him he needed to get out of the office and enjoy life. He'd thought maybe he needed to find a woman to distract himself with for a while. After all, what was a padded wallet good for but to pull out and attract the next shiny thing?

When Sterling called and asked him to meet him and Sayla in Jackson for Christmas and New Year's, he'd been happy. He was going to spend a traditional Christmas with family. He'd been so happy he'd decided to spend a week in Park City first, where his mom and dad used to take them every December when he and his brother were younger. Maybe it was time to do more than have a distraction in his life. Maybe now he needed a real relationship, something like his brother had.

Determined to thoroughly enjoy this week, he'd spent the day skiing. It'd been an incredible rush. Now, his aching back and legs were begging to be done, so he told himself he would do this last run and then go back to his resort and take a soak in the hot tub.

"On your right!" Someone shouted behind him.

Looking over his shoulder, he saw a neon-pink coat, gloves, and a hat coming at him.

Trying to scoot out of the way, he thought the woman would hit him, but at the last minute, she curved to the side, barely missing him. She did some kind of move that sprayed snow in his face.

"This is the *fast track*!" She yelled. "Stay out of the way!"

Fuming, he pushed off and decided right then to stay on her heels all the way down the mountain and give her a piece of his mind. After all, this was *his* vacation, and he had been having a pretty good time before this clearly insane woman got in his way. What nerve or right did the pink-fleeced snow bunny have telling him to get out of *her* way? And *fast track*? Who said a person couldn't take a minute at the top of a mountain to enjoy the view?

The faster he went, bending into the run and putting his poles closer to his sides, the farther the woman seemed to get away from him—which was insane because he was flying down the mountain. Skiing was something he was passionate about and had made time to do four or five times a year all through his life. It was pure joy to him.

By the time he arrived at the bottom of the mountain, the pink woman was gone. Searching the exit, he couldn't spot her. Man, the woman had been fast. And rude. He was seething just thinking about her, but he consoled himself with the thought of going back to the resort and letting his problems melt away in the hot tub.

Sitting, he tugged off his skis then walked in the jilted way skiers walk with the boots on. At the lodge, he checked in his gear before changing into his hiking boots and heading toward his room. Scanning the shops along the edges of the resort, he considered his options for dinner. It was even more difficult to choose because he couldn't decide if he should eat first or if he could wait until he'd soaked his sore muscles in the hot tub. Which problem was worse, his screaming muscles or the nagging hunger?

He came to a stop when he saw the woman in pink gear standing next to a booth. The ski resort had set up little tent shops in part of the parking lot. It looked like there were a variety of vendors. They had everything from new sports labels hoping to make it big to the mainstream brands everyone knew. There were also boutique-like tents with local crafts that people could buy for souvenirs or last-minute Christmas gifts.

His heart skipped a beat as she took off her helmet and her blond curls fell around her face. When he looked closer, he saw she was talking on her cell phone.

Perfect. He would get a chance to give her a piece of his mind after all.

Someone walked out of the tent next to her and turned to her. "Night, boss, you sure you're okay to close up alone?"

He saw her shake her head.

"Yep, see ya." She put her phone down. Then turned around, startling him. Seeing the tears in her eyes and the tense expression on her face, he stopped abruptly.

Without knowing why, he asked, "What's wrong?"

She focused intensely on his face and gave him an incredulous, confused look. "Do I know you?"

"No." It made no sense given a minute ago he was ready to give her a piece of his mind, but he felt drawn to her. Maybe she was exactly the distraction he needed during this trip. "Unless you call almost knocking me down up there on the mountain our first date." He attempted a charming smirk.

She frowned and shook her head, blinking away the tears. "Oh, you were the *idiot* in everyone's way at the top of the mountain up there."

Being called an idiot right to his face didn't happen that often to Nathan Pennington. "Right, you're on the *fast track*, and I need to get out of the way." He made air quotes for her benefit.

Narrowing her eyes, she said, "Listen, tonight's not the night to mess with me." She pinched the bridge of her nose. "I don't know who you are, and I don't know what you want, but just stay out of my way."

What he wanted very much was to get in her way, but she was already stalking over to the table piled high with neon-colored products much like the ones she was wearing. Giving the whole thing a once-over, with the hangers laid out over the bundles of things and the bins out, he figured she was putting stuff away for the night.

"Is this some type of trade show or something?" he asked. Her shop was one of the many tents in the parking lot outside of the regular shops.

She didn't respond.

"Excuse me?" Nathan wasn't used to being ignored either.

Letting out a sigh, she picked up a sweatshirt and folded it. "This is an expo for all the latest and greatest in new products coming out on the market. Park City Resort puts it on for a few days before Christmas every year so all the richies can be wowed and buy the best stuff." She snorted and slipped something into a bin beneath the table, not looking at him.

Turning around, he took in the large quantity of products she had. "So you're trying to unload all this over the next couple of days?"

"Wow, you're a genius."

He stared at her, nonplussed. "O-kay." Man, this really wasn't turning out to be the distraction he was looking for.

Continuing the process of pulling sweatshirts, jackets, and a plethora of other gear off the table and into bins, she said, "I would say 'don't let the door hit you on the way out' if I had a door, but obviously I don't."

This woman had issues. Anger issues mostly. Yet when he'd first seen her get off the phone, he could have sworn she was about to cry. Not knowing what compelled him to do it, he moved to the men's gear and picked up a coat, noticing the brand name was FastTrack. "Clever. Your brand name is the same thing you used to insult me."

She glared at him then continued packing up gear.

Eyeing the gear, unsure why he cared so much, he asked, "Will it keep me warm all day on the slopes? And at night?" He studied a pair of black gloves for a moment before reaching out and feeling the material.

She hesitated and then cleared her throat. "Yes."

He liked the fact that she clearly wasn't the kind of person who turned on the salesman charm instantly. It was sad for her in a business sense, but in general, it was a good trait to have on a personal level. It made her seem more authentic. He pulled his wallet out of his coat. "I'll take a complete set of gear. Coat, hat, gloves, and pants. All in black."

Her jaw dropped, but she collected herself and crossed her arms like she didn't trust him. "Why?"

He shot her a stern look then moved his gaze back to the gear, sizing up the quality of the coat's workmanship. "The correct response is 'Great, awesome customer, I'll get that ready for you.'" He knew he sounded condescending, but he didn't care. The more he inspected the product, the more he liked it.

"Who are you?"

Casually, he pulled out a credit card and took a step toward her, finally meeting her eyes. They were the bluest eyes he'd ever seen. They reminded him of the Cayman Islands where he'd gone diving two years ago.

When he didn't answer, she cocked her head to the side. "Seriously, who are you? Someone famous? Some millionaire visiting Park City?" She snorted.

He gave her a quizzical look. "Why do you care? I want to purchase your merchandise. Isn't that enough?"

She shrugged. "Don't be offended that I don't know you. I don't watch television."

Mimicking her expression, he asked, "Who are you? Someone famous? Don't be offended. I don't watch television either." It bothered him he was acting petty, but the words just came out.

Giving him a glare, she took his credit card and turned to run it in her machine. "You know this isn't cheap. The product is the best in blended fabrics. It whisks away moisture, keeping you cool and dry."

"You've run my card. You don't need to give me a sales presentation now." He kept his words calm.

She matched his glare, and her nostrils flared. "I just want you to know this stuff is quality. I want you to *appreciate* it." She handed his card back to him.

Not having any idea why he seemed to be at odds with this beautiful woman, he shook his head and watched as she packaged up all of his gear.

She sized him up. "Are you a men's large?"

Hesitating briefly, he nodded. "Yep." He watched as she folded his gear quickly, noting how she took pride in her stock. "You know, you might be able to sell more items if you smiled once in a while."

She didn't pause in her folding. "Thanks for the unsolicited sales tip." She flashed him the same mocking kind of smile he'd given her. "But I already sold to you, didn't I?"

He let out a light laugh. "Fair enough."

She shoved all his stuff into a bag and thrust it at him.

Taking it, he grinned. "Hey, truly, you'd sell more if you smiled and even pretended to be happy you were selling the gear." It was funny to him that he wanted to tease her, pester her. Even if she wouldn't engage out of politeness, he still wanted to draw out some kind of reaction.

She ripped off the receipt, glanced at it, then put on an overly fake smile. "Here you go, Mr. Pennington. Have a great day."

As he took the receipt, their hands brushed. Ungloved hands. Somehow it felt more intimate than he knew it was.

Letting go of the bag, she held his gaze. "You can leave now."

Now that he had her reacting, he ratcheted up his intensity level. "Is this part of your fast track mentality? Get the customer in, get the customer out? If I were you, I'd be trying to upsell me. Maybe offer me a set of skis." He eyed the skis on the ground.

Scoffing, she turned back to packing stuff up. "I'm in a hurry, okay?"

"Right, fast track, I forgot." Man, why couldn't he just walk away? "All I can tell you from personal experience is sometimes the fast track part of life is way overrated."

Mid-packing a coat into a bin, she eyed him. "Yeah, people at the end of the fast track always say that."

He frowned. "They may mean it too."

She sputtered out a laugh. "Ya know, I just got off the phone with the guy who is supposed to fund me. The guy who promised he would put my products in mainstream stores—good stores like Eddie Bauer and REI—just told me if I don't push seventy percent of the rest of this merchandise tomorrow on the big expo day, he's going to drop me. Unfortunately for me, I don't know how that's gonna happen." Once again, he saw tears in her eyes. "So don't stand here and give me life lessons, okay? When people like you already have their millions, they can say anything they want."

He decided not to correct her statement by informing her he was a billionaire. Instead, he turned for the tent opening.

She sighed. "I'm sorry. Look, it's just been one of those days, okay?"

He turned back.

She shook her head and reached for another coat, letting out a derisive laugh. "It's kinda been one of those years to tell you the truth."

He paused and then moved back, offering his hand. "Let's start over. I'm Nathan."

Letting out a puff of air, she looked at his hand, but shook her head.

"Really, let's start over. I'm Nathan." He insisted.

"You're not going to leave until I give you my name, are you?"

He had to smile at her brashness, her sarcasm with a bit of pissed off sprinkled in. Every woman he'd dated for the past few years had been the political type—polished, schooled in the right topics, dressed in the right clothes, and they always said the right things. This woman was refreshing. "Nope, not gonna leave without a name."

Shaking his hand, she gave him a little smile. "I'm Storm."

Oh yeah, that fit her.

She pulled back. "And I'm not in the mood for weather jokes, okay? My mother grew up here and was fascinated by the storms that blew through."

The information interested him, but he didn't push her. "Nice to meet you."

She studied him for a moment before grinning. "Man, that's a practiced smile." Cocking her head to the side, she lifted an eyebrow. "Completely fake."

Finding all thoughts of aches and pains and hunger gone, he realized he wanted to know more about her. "Really?"

"Completely."

"How do you know?"

She gestured to him. "'Cause I've been talking to you, and I've seen the real one." She stuck her chin out. "When you were teasing me. Now it looks like you're running for president."

Thoughts of his father flashed through his mind. His gut twisted, and he felt himself wincing.

"I'm sorry." She was giving him an intense look.

He quickly changed the subject. "Tell me about this bad day or year."

A derisive laugh escaped her as she opened another bin and loaded more merchandise into it. "Ah, no. It's … complicated."

Taking a chance, he put his bag of stuff down and moved next to her, folding one of the coats the way she was doing.

She shook her head, but kept packing. "Now you're helping me?"

"Why not?" He leaned over the table and put it neatly in her bin. Then he reached for another. "It's the Christmas spirit, right?"

Lifting her eyebrows, she put another coat in the bin and closed it. "So you're a Mr. Do-Gooder, are you?"

He was the completely opposite kind of guy, and he knew it, but he just grinned and said, "Yep, that's me."

"Hmm." She worked fast, closing the bin he'd been working on and then shifting her focus to gathering another bin labeled 'gloves.' "I guess you can do what you want. It's a free country."

Liking that she wasn't arguing with him, and liking even more that this day had taken quite the turn, he closed the bin and reached for another one labeled 'socks.' "You didn't sell me socks."

She shot him a curt glance. "You need socks?"

"Maybe." He grinned. "I guess I'll have to come back tomorrow on your big merchandise pushing day and buy some."

She shook her head, her face falling. "I don't know how I'm going to do what Ken wants. I won't even be able to start selling until after lunch; I have to work in the morning."

Looking at all the work she was doing, he couldn't stop himself from asking, "Where do you work during the day?"

She picked up her phone and looked at the time. "I have to hurry." She shoved more stuff into a bin.

He picked up the pace. "Where do you work?"

"Uh, I was an Olympic skier." She frowned. "Hurt my knee, blah blah blah, ended up not being good enough for the Olympics to take me a second time, but good enough to do shoots for products. Magazine covers." She shrugged. "Not my products, unfortunately. Haven't figured out how to finance that yet. I'm hoping something works out soon."

He could swear he saw her lip tremble.

"Something has to." She whispered. She filled the last bin, turned for the snowboards, and paused.

"Where are you going tonight?"

Glancing briefly at him, she frowned. "Are you always this pushy with a girl you just met?"

Caught, he smiled. "Nope."

Squinting at him, she asked, "So what's your deal? Are you just here to ski?"

He nodded, unsure why he was suddenly nervous. "Yep, here until Christmas. Then I'm going to stay with my brother and new sister-in-law."

"New sister-in-law?"

"Yep." He remembered Sterling and Sayla's wedding in Jackson. His father had been there. It'd been a perfect day. He frowned, thinking of how, less than a month later, his father had passed away. They'd known about his heart, but it had never seemed possible he'd ever be gone.

"So you get to ski for five days?" Pure jealousy was written all over her face. "Then go on vacation?"

Shaken from his thoughts, he put on his best real smile. "Yep."

"What's wrong with you?"

"What do you mean?"

She looked him up and down. "I don't know. You seem manic. You're fake happy. Then there are these slivers of pain in your eyes."

He looked away. "It's nothing."

She sighed. "Okay, never mind. I have enough of my own junk to handle."

They were both quiet for a few seconds. He tried to shake this intense feeling between them. She'd been the first person to ever notice his moods. Strike that—she'd been the first to call him on it. He wondered if others were simply afraid to. Purposefully, he changed the topic. "Hey, you live here and probably ski or snowboard every day."

She let slip a sarcastic laugh. "Well, yeah, but that's mixed into work."

"Still." He countered. "You live here."

"Not in Park City." She turned away, looking sad.

"Where?"

"Uh, no. I don't tell people where I live. No stalkers, thanks."

He laughed. "Yeah." Little did she know he could make one call and find out anything he wanted to know about her from his contacts in less than ten minutes. That was the benefit of having to background check people for a life in politics.

He didn't know what to say, but could tell she was holding something back which was ludicrous because he'd just met her. "I don't need to stalk women." It was the truth, but it sounded like he was at a bad political debate defending himself.

He didn't have to say anything because the look in her eye let him know he was going to regret pestering her. "Do you mind helping me load all this into my truck? Since you're a *do-gooder* and all?"

Her tone made him smile. He thought about how he'd actually forgotten how hungry and sore he was since meeting her. Man oh man, he didn't understand how he'd gotten so lucky. "Sure, but only if you let me buy you dinner."

She headed down the sidewalk. "Can't tonight." She called back. "Like I said, I have somewhere I have to be."

He watched her jog to the parking lot and realized the more she said, the more he wanted to know about her. The Olympics? Her injury? And the number one question rattling around in his brain: was she married? Or did she have a boyfriend?

A few minutes later, she pulled up and kept the truck running as they quickly loaded the bins and gear. Once they finished, he shut the tailgate and turned to her. "So will you let me take you out to dinner *tomorrow* night?" He tried not to sound too hopeful.

She moved to the driver's side door then paused. "Don't date out-of-towners. Sorry." She gave a mock smile. "I'm not the 'hang around the slopes and wait for a rich guy' type."

Man, he was liking this woman more and more.

She got into her truck and rolled down the window. "But I do appreciate the help."

"You're going to be here tomorrow, right?"

She crossed her arms. "I told you, no stalkers."

He laughed.

She grinned and said somewhat reluctantly, "I have a shoot tomorrow, but I will open the tent doors at one." Putting her hands on the wheel, she looked thoughtful. "Thanks for your help. Maybe you can stop and give me some more sales tips another time."

Not believing he was doing this, he put his hand on the window. "Wait, let's make a deal. I'll show up and help you sell your merchandise. If I sell more than you, I take you to dinner."

She gave him a doubtful look. "You're going to help me sell merchandise, and if *you* do better than *me*, you take *me* to dinner?"

He shrugged. "It's a win-win for you."

When she bit her bottom lip, he couldn't help but think how pretty her heart-shaped face was. "C'mon, it'll be fun."

Both eyebrows rose. "What do you get out of this?"

He shrugged. "Oh, believe me, my ego will get plenty out of outselling you after you put me in the dust on the slope earlier."

She tried to hide a smile.

"C'mon." He pressed.

She spread her hands in a gesture of mock defeat. "What can I say? I need the help as you've clearly pointed out. Since you're so good with all the sales tips, I guess we'll see if you're as good of a salesman."

"All right then. It's a date."

She laughed. "I wouldn't call it a date."

"Fast track, right? If you believe it, you can achieve it. I know I can outsell you." He grinned, feeling cocky. "I'll bet you I can outsell you and whoever else you want to bring too."

She rolled up the window. "Fine." She winked at him. "Okay, I guess you'll put up or shut up. See you tomorrow afternoon at two."

"Two? I thought you opened at one?"

She shrugged. "Give me time to set up. Plus, skiers are usually done skiing between two and five. It gets too dark."

"Sounds good." Nathan watched her drive away, and a wide grin spread across his face. This could be an interesting couple of days after all. He took off, heading back in the direction of the hotel attached to the resort. The night was still young, and he felt good enough to skip the hot tub, take a shower, and go out and find another pretty smile with his dinner. This was gonna be a good trip. He could feel it.

Purchase HERE!